NIGHT RIDING

NIGHT RIDING

by
KATHERINE
MARTIN

ALFRED A. KNOPF ❧ NEW YORK

This Is a Borzoi Book
Published by Alfred A. Knopf, Inc.

Copyright © 1989 by Katherine McConnell Martin
Jacket illustration copyright © 1989 by Allen Garns
All rights reserved under International and Pan-American Copyright
Conventions. Published in the United States by Alfred A. Knopf, Inc.,
New York, and simultaneously in Canada by Random House of Canada
Limited, Toronto. Distributed by Random House, Inc., New York.
Manufactured in the United States of America
Book design by Elizabeth Hardie

2   4   6   8   0   9   7   5   3   1

Library of Congress Cataloging-in-Publication Data
Martin, Katherine McConnell. Night riding.
Summary: Eleven-year-old Prin's secure world in a small
Tennessee town during the 1950s is turned upside down when she
discovers that her new friend and neighbor is being abused by
the girl's own father.
ISBN 0-679-80064-6 ISBN 0-679-90064-0 (lib. bdg.)
[1. Friendship—Fiction. 2. Child molesting—Fiction.
3. Incest—Fiction. 4. Fathers and daughters—Fiction.
5. Tennessee—Fiction] I. Title.   PZ7.M36335Ni   1989
[Fic]   89-2711

To Syble, who, like Ada Ruth, held it all together

NIGHT RIDING

One

MARY FAITH HAMMOND moved in next door the seventeenth of May, two days after school let out and the same day we found out Daddy was sick.

Around noon Mama and Daddy went to the doctor's, leaving me and Jo Lynn home alone for the first time ever. As soon as their car made the turn down our driveway, I told Jo Lynn not to try to boss me around just because she was fifteen and I was eleven. Then I went to the barn and saddled up Flash, planning to ride all the way around Otwell's Lakes.

But halfway up our driveway Flash suddenly jumped sideways a few steps, nearly throwing me off. After I got my balance, I saw what had scared her: a girl stood among the pine trees along our fence line. She was tall, about my sister's age, and wore short shorts and a loose white blouse with a scooped neck and no sleeves. Her hair was long and blond, and heavy black lines were drawn around her eyes and straight back to her hairline, like an Egyptian lady.

"What are you staring at?" is what she said.

"You like to scared my horse to death, jumping out that way. She almost threw me into the barbed wire."

"I's just standing here. I didn't jump out of any-wheres."

"Well you're trespassing on our property. Where'd you come from?"

She jerked her head toward the path behind her, and the rusty iron gate set in the fence between us and the old Thompson place. It had been forced open, and where she'd walked the weeds had a silver-headed, disturbed look. "We're moving in today. I'm your new neighbor." She stretched her mouth in a smile that didn't get to her eyes.

"What's your name?" I said.

"That's for me to know and you to find out."

"If you don't want to talk to anybody, you can just go on home."

"I reckon I'll go where I want. It'll take more than you to stop me."

I opened my mouth to tell her my Daddy could, but she'd decided to be friendly. "Is this your horse?" she asked, walking toward us with her hand out to pet Flash. "Kind of small, ain't it?"

"I've got another one, a bay mare named Lady that can run faster than anything you've ever seen," I answered.

"Why aren't you riding her?"

"I wanted to ride Flash," I said, not about to tell her I couldn't always make Lady behave.

Up close, I saw the girl's face had a dirty, purple-yellow bruise underneath the black lines drawn around her right eye.

"I had a black eye once," I said. "Flash here swung her head around and popped me good right under my eye—stayed black for a week. How'd you get yours?"

"I don't have a black eye. That's just a bad makeup job I hadn't washed off yet."

I snorted. "Well, it *looks* like a black eye," I said, turning Flash toward the gate.

"I sure would like to ride," she piped up.

I frowned and opened my mouth to say no. But right then a man's voice called from beyond the pines, "Mary Faith, you git back here and git to work before I take a belt to you." The voice was mean, and the girl jumped, then turned and shoved through the gate, leaving it open behind her.

I tied Flash to the fence and crawled into a little cave among the pine trees, where I could watch what was going on next door. The girl, a man, and a boy who looked about eighteen were moving things into the house from a beat-up old truck. The boy carried a basketball back and forth three times before the man yelled for him to put the damn thing down and give a hand with the moving. The man was small and seemed lazy, spending most of his time telling the boy and girl what to do.

I watched for a while, but it was hot and nobody cursed again or did anything else interesting, so I backed out of the cave and headed home, anxious to tell Jo Lynn about our new neighbors.

But before I was halfway there, she came running out the kitchen door looking for me.

"Hurry up—Mama's on the phone," she called.

I had dust and pine needles on my feet, so I'd leave footprints on Mama's floors, but Jo Lynn didn't give me time to wipe them off. She pulled me inside and followed me to the hall, where our telephone sat in a little box in the wall. I took the heavy receiver and turned my back so she couldn't listen.

"Yes, ma'am?" I said.

"Speak up, Prin—I can hardly hear you." Mama's voice was high.

"*Yes*, ma'am?"

"I have something to tell you," Mama said, in the calm, false voice she uses to warn me there's a snake nearby. My heart speeded up. "I want you not to worry now, because everything'll be all right. It's Daddy." She waited a minute.

"Yes, ma'am?" I said.

"Daddy's sick," she said. "We just found that out from the doctor; he's going to have to go to the hospital. He'll be all right, but he'll be away for a while."

She stopped again, but I didn't have anything to say.

"Now what I want you to do is play like you always do. I'll be home later on and tell you all about it. You do what Jo Lynn says."

I said yes, ma'am again.

"Put her on the phone. I love you, Prin."

"Mama wants to talk to you," I said to my sister, handing her the receiver. Before she put it to her ear, I said, "I'm going to the barn," and went out the back door.

I felt like a glass jar had dropped around me and stopped time. I barely remembered to unsaddle Flash, and I forgot about the new people next door. All I could think about was Daddy.

ABOUT DUSK MAMA came home alone. By the look on her face I knew Daddy wasn't coming back for a long time. He was just gone, disappeared into the West Tennessee Tuberculosis Hospital, where visiting hours were on Wednesday nights and Sunday afternoons for anybody over twelve.

My daddy is a horseman. He sits a horse easy, and it doesn't do anything but what he wants. He's not afraid of Big Red, the sorrel gelding as tall at the shoulder as he is, or of Lady, the bay mare he brought home when he thought I had learned all I could from riding Flash.

The first time I rode her, Lady ran away with me. She clamped down on the bit and bolted toward the barn, stirrups beating her sides and me holding on to the saddle horn yelling for help. I was scared to death, knowing I'd have to jump or be scraped off at the low barn door.

But I didn't have to jump. Daddy ran out of the barn and grabbed Lady's bridle, his heels digging in and his weight yanking her head down. When she stopped, I was hanging off the side of her neck.

As soon as she was quiet, I swung down and walked away, still scared, and ashamed I'd let go of the reins to hold on to the saddle horn.

"Come get back on, Princess," Daddy called.

"She's too much horse for me—I can't hold her."

"Yes, you can. You can't let yourself be afraid, Prin, because a horse'll know it, and use it against you every time you ride. Get back on. I'll ride with you."

I did what Daddy said, trembling as bad as Lady, and followed him and Red down to the back pasture. Daddy kept up a running talk, showing me how to use my knees and a soft pressure on the reins to tell Lady what to do. Before the afternoon was over, she and I were easy with each other, racing through the wind behind Daddy and Big Red.

The night Daddy didn't come home, the horses ran. They rolled like thunder from the bottom pasture up to the barn, through the narrowing by the water trough, and on to the high front pasture. Their hoofbeats grew far and soft, thudding across the field where Daddy and I laid out a baseball diamond, down the driveway fence, then under my window again.

When I heard them coming back, I rolled over in my top bunk and watched out the window for them. I knew their heads would be high and their nostrils blown out square, their tails blowing behind, all silver and black shadows flying through the night. I listened to them, listened to Mama trying to get settled in her and Daddy's bedroom next door, and wished I was night riding, feeling the weeds stinging my legs, the wind rushing along the hair on my arms, cool even on a hot night. I bet Daddy would have liked to have been with us, night riding, too.

I STAYED AWAKE too long. In the morning I was sleepy and couldn't get going. Even in summer Mama wakes everybody early so we can do our chores before it gets hot.

Mama had the living room curtains down, the furniture shoved out from the walls, and a pile of clean rags on the floor by the door. It was painting day.

I walked through the living room and out the kitchen door, looking first for snakes on the patio. The tiles and the iron frame of our swing were clean and fresh with a cool morning feel. Up off our high pasture a light mist was rising; the horses were grazing in the valley.

"Breakfast, Prin."

"I'm not hungry."

"Come eat."

I went back inside, where Jo Lynn was already sitting down. She was wearing blue jeans and an old shirt, but had her hair tied back in a ribbon and color pinched into her cheeks. Mama didn't sit with us, just washed up her coffee cup and took some meat out of the refrigerator.

"The horses were restless last night," she said. I smiled. "I don't want you fooling with Lady until your daddy gets home. You ride Flash."

"Mama—"

"Soon as you finish up breakfast, get started painting." Mama looked out the window over the sink, then around the kitchen like she was following a fly. "The living room's to be painted this summer, and that's what we're going to do."

"I'm supposed to go to Margaret's," Jo Lynn said.

"I want to go swimming," I said.

"Work in the mornings, play in the afternoons," Mama said. "But no more swimming in the lake."

"Why not?"

"Because I said so." Then she sighed. "Anyway, who's to go with you now? Who's going to be watching in case you get in trouble?"

Jo Lynn and I looked at her.

Mama looked out the window again, at the horses. "I can tell you something right now," she said, pulling out a chair and sitting with her arms folded, a hand cupped around each elbow. "It'll be a lot harder with Daddy gone. You two will have to do more work and there'll be less play and less money." She was looking at Jo Lynn.

"We'll be all right, because Daddy had good benefits at the railroad, and the hospital'll take him almost free. But it'll be different. I'll have to learn to do his work with the trucks."

"How long is Daddy going to be sick?" I said.

"I don't know. They caught him early, but I think it'll be a while. They're running tests," she said. One hand rubbed her stomach; her belt buckle lay almost flat up, like it was holding her stomach down, the opposite of men whose buckles make a sling to hold their bellies up.

"What'll they do to him in the hospital?" Jo Lynn said.

"Mostly he'll rest. Tuberculosis is something in the lungs that makes it hard to breathe, makes you weak. Your grandmama had it, too, back when they didn't know how to do for it." Her eyes went to the window again.

"She died from it," Jo Lynn said.

"That was a long time ago, before you were born," Mama said. "This is 1958, and there's all kinds of things they can do now, medicines and rest."

"Why can't he rest here?" I said.

"Because TB is catching. Everything he touches you can catch it from, so he can't stay here and maybe us get it."

"What if we've already got it?"

"We don't. We're going to the mobile unit right after lunch and be x-rayed, though. Every month for a while we'll be x-rayed, just checking, to be sure we don't get it from something."

"I'm supposed to go to Margaret's," Jo Lynn said, loud.

"I'll drop you off after the x-rays if you've already made promises. But don't you do it again without asking. This is going to be a work summer."

"That's all we ever do," Jo Lynn said.

"There'll be one good, special thing for each of you this summer," Mama said. "I want you to think carefully about what you want, just one thing, something we can afford."

"What about the baby?" Jo Lynn said. "What're we going to do about your having the baby?"

"Have it," Mama said. She looked surprised.

"Will you get to teach next year?"

But Mama was getting up from the table. "That's then," she said. "This is now.

"You be sure that paint's stirred up good," she told Jo Lynn, already on her way across the living room. "Start in a corner. We're going on just like nothing's changed."

Two

I BOUNCED MY spoon on my oatmeal, picked it up like a piece of bowl-shaped rubber, and licked the sugar off the top.

"You're disgusting," Jo Lynn said. She put her bowl and glass in the sink and slammed out the door toward the old garage, a place she hated. It was musty and dark, fastened on to the back of the new office and big screened porch Daddy had finished building not a month ago.

I followed; we both stopped just inside the door

to let our eyes learn to see in the darker light. "I hate summers," she said, pulling a gallon of paint to the edge of the shelf. "There's nothing to do but work, nobody for miles." She hunted for Daddy's screwdriver and pried off the lid.

"There is now," I said, remembering our new neighbors. "Somebody's moving into the old Thompson place."

"Who'd live in that rat trap?"

"The girl's name is Mary Faith. She's about your age, but I haven't seen her around before. There's a man and a boy, too."

"The Hammonds?" Jo Lynn squeaked, her eyes round. "The Hammonds are moving in next door?"

I shrugged.

"I can't live next door to Mary Faith Hammond," she whispered. "She *can't* live there."

"What's wrong with Mary Faith Hammond?"

She snorted, acting old and superior again. "You don't need to know, Miss Nosybody. Just stick to your horses."

"You can tell me. I promise I won't tell a soul," I said, getting real interested.

"I'd stick to my horses if I were you," she repeated, her face taking on a mean look. "After all, you may not have them too much longer."

"Why not?" I asked, alarmed enough to forget about Mary Faith.

"Horses don't do anything but cost money. How are we going to pay for them now, with Mama and Daddy neither one working?"

"They're paid for," I said. "And Mama never works in the summer."

"Their hooves have to be trimmed," she said, hunting for paintbrushes. "There's oats, and bridles and all that folderol. Something's always breaking."

I shrugged, deciding she was just trying to aggravate me.

"You don't see it, do you?" she said, as she handed me a stack of newspapers to carry. "You don't know what it means for Dad to be sick maybe a long time, maybe forever, maybe even die! And Mama's having a baby. She can't teach school with a baby."

"Why not?"

"They don't let expecting ladies teach. And then who's going to take care of it? You and me have to go to school."

"I don't know," I said. I was tired of her talking about things I couldn't do anything about. "Mama'll fix it."

Jo Lynn slammed an old paintbrush against the door frame to loosen up its bristles. "Mama can't fix everything," she said.

I turned my back on Jo Lynn and left, watching so I wouldn't stub my toes on the stepping stones through the flowers. Jo Lynn was always looking for the bad side of things. She didn't like the horses, or our house, or living in the country. She probably wouldn't even have stayed if Mama hadn't made her a red satin suit and let her be a majorette at Bartlett High School.

IN THE LIVING room I spread newspaper along the front wall, starting under the window, where the sofa was shoved out. Our walls were spackled, heavy spackling that had interesting shapes, like the peaks of ice cream cones. Nobody in the family but me like spackled walls, but they were going to be hard to paint.

Mama had been planning on painting since back in March, when she found out about the baby and decided to wait to build our new house. I'd heard her and Daddy talk about the baby in their bedroom next to mine. "Why now?" Mama had said. "We're just about to see daylight; now we'll have to put off building till I get back to work. I'm too old to go through diapers again."

"You've got two girls to help you this time," Daddy said, and coughed. "We'll make it just fine, if we're careful."

"We can't save anything on only one salary." Mama sounded scared. "And what if there're complications? What if they don't hold my job, or I have to go all the way to Memphis, to a city school?"

"You're a good teacher—they'll not want to lose you."

"I don't have any seniority in Raleigh Springs."

There was silence a time; then Daddy coughed again.

"When are you going to see about that cough?" she asked. Then, "I don't think I can stand to live another year in this excuse for a house."

"Well, you don't have to have a baby, you know. We've got the girls, and if it's going to upset everything that much, we just won't have another one."

"How can you say such a thing!" Mama's bare feet slapped against the hall floor on her way to the bathroom. I listened to her brush her teeth, heard Daddy cough and hawk and spit, heard his trousers drop to the floor, and after a while my shoulders and breath eased up a little.

When Mama came back from the bathroom, her

voice was smiling like an apology. "Margaret Ann asked me what I thought I was doing having a baby at my time of life," she said.

"If Margaret Ann had had one herself, it'd have improved her disposition one hundred percent."

Mama laughed. "It's going to make a big difference, you know," she said. "I hope it's a boy."

"It won't matter what it is," Daddy said. "We've got Prin."

"Prin's a girl," Mama said. "Sooner or later she'll want to act like one."

THE COMMERCIAL APPEAL I spread out under the windows had drawings of women in Sunday dresses with fitted tops and big, flaring skirts over petticoats. They wore white gloves and flat-brimmed hats on the very tops of their heads, and held little black purses. On the other side of the page was a drawing of a man in a Robert Hall suit with pleated pants, the crease dented a little just above his shoe. The man's hat had a narrower brim than the women's.

Dad could dress like that picture and look good, like a suit belonged on him. But if Mama wore a tight top and a big skirt, she'd look short and fat. Aunt Map could pull it off, though. She was tall and skinny and wore Kay Windsor dresses with clean white gloves.

My thinking about Map must have called her up: it wasn't any time before she pulled down our driveway in her big yellow Buick.

"Oh, Lord," Mama said, looking out the naked windows. "Just what I need this morning."

She held open the screen door, and Map walked into our living room like it was hers. "You should have called yesterday," she said right off. "How come you didn't call me?"

"Everything was taken care of," Mama said. "Let's get ourselves some tea and sit on the porch."

Aunt Map looked at the newspaper and the paint Jo Lynn was pouring into a little bucket for me, and her top lip tucked under so that wrinkles shot out in all directions.

"I just feel so sorry for you," she told Mama, following her to the kitchen. "Just when things were looking up. I told you—"

"Here's your tea." Some sloshed on Map's white gloves. Mama turned to us. "You finish that wall before lunch. We have to be at the x-ray unit at one o'clock." She held the door open for Map.

Map is our only relation—her name is Margaret Ann Porter. Mama's dead brother was her husband. She has lived in Raleigh Springs her whole life and knows everybody, but drives all the way into Memphis to teach English and the social graces at Tredwell High School. Map wears flat, rubber-soled shoes because she has bunions; the lenses of her glasses are cut in half, so her eyes jump forward and back, or multiply, when she looks at you through the top or bottom parts.

She and Mama sat in the white wicker armchairs on the front porch, and I switched from painting under the windows to painting right by the door.

"I don't know what it is that you've done, Ada Ruth, that all this is visited on you. Having a baby at your time of life, now Brian's sick, and the most disreputable family in Raleigh Springs moving in next door."

"Who's moving in?" Mama frowned at her.

"The B.Z. Hammonds."

Jo Lynn groaned, then put her brush down and tiptoed over to the door. I made her stand behind me so I could still hear everything. "I always thought you were personally a good woman," Map said, shaking her head over the glass of tea like she was enjoying a piece of divinity caught in her teeth.

"A baby's a blessing. And you know that isn't the way things work, Margaret Ann," Mama said.

"Well, you can't deny having white trash move in next door isn't trouble," Map said, sniffing. "There've been rumors about B.Z. Hammond since I can't remember when, everything from beating his wife to—"

"Shu-u-u," Mama hissed, jerking her head toward the living room.

I leaned closer to the door.

Map dropped her voice to a whisper that was just loud enough to hear. "And every Hammond girl I ever heard of has been pregnant by the time she was sixteen. Mary Faith's just the latest in a long line."

At first I was interested that Map had said *pregnant* instead of *expecting* like me and Jo Lynn were supposed to. Then it hit me: the girl I'd met yesterday was going to have a baby! Jo Lynn's hand flew over my mouth just in time to stop me from saying, "Wow!"

"There's more," Map went on. "Guess who's bought that skinny little piece of land by you, Otwell's side?"

"Who?"

"Mose Hardy."

"I've never heard anything against Mose. He's a churchgoing man."

I nodded, remembering how Mr. Mose and Daddy stood outside smoking between Sunday school and church. Daddy liked Mr. Mose, saying he was the best builder in Raleigh Springs.

"I can't figure why he'd build his own house on that little piece of land when he can afford to live anywhere he wants," Map was saying.

"I don't want to talk about other people's problems today. I have enough of my own," Mama said, sounding tired.

Map was quiet for about half a minute.

"That's why I'm here," she said. "To offer you some constructive advice. You're going to need help."

"I'll call when I do."

"Now, I've talked it over with Ed Lewis at the bank, and we agree that the trucks have to go—"

"No."

"Hear me out." Map put her tea glass down and leaned forward, her elbows on the wings of the wicker chair.

"You know I've got good business sense—you listen to what I say. Dump trucking is no work for a woman. Nobody's going to want to do business with you, no more than they have to, to be polite. What do you know about trucking?"

The whole time Map was talking, Mama's face worked itself around in shapes I'd never seen before. When she answered Map, she sounded like she looked—scared. "I've helped Brian all along; I've done all of the bookkeeping. And those trucks are our future. Just how do you think we got ahead? It sure wasn't on a railroad and a teaching salary!"

But Map kept right on, not having enough sense to try to calm Mama down first. "Brian was working himself to death with two jobs. You take the trucking on, you'll wind up like he has. How long do you think you can hold out? Use your common sense, Ada Ruth. You won't be teaching school this fall, and Brian's not going to be working for a long time. Not trucking. Not the railroad."

"We have the house savings. I can pay the bills through the summer. Then I'll do what I have to. Until then"—Mama stood and picked up both tea glasses—"I'd appreciate your just letting me call you when I need to." Her voice was tight as a whip. Jo Lynn and I jumped back and started painting.

"You try to hold out through the summer, you'll

lose everything." Map followed Mama in the door. "Sell those trucks right now."

"How do you like that color blue?" Mama said. "There's a discolored place under the window I didn't know about. Must be a leak somewhere."

"Are you listening to a thing I say?" Map said.

"I'm trying my best not to."

I laughed.

"What are you laughing at, Miss Priss?" Map said, but Mama had her by the arm, steering her out the door.

They stood by her car talking awhile, Mama with her arms folded across her stomach. Then she waved Map off and stood a minute longer, looking the house over from one end to the other. She walked back to the porch slow, her head down, something painful about her so that I didn't watch anymore, but painted the discolored spot under the window its second coat, which it still showed through.

Three

WHEN WE GOT back from x-ray, I went down to the pasture with an apple to catch Flash. There were two things I wanted to do. One was to ride over and see what Mr. Mose Hardy from our church was going to do with that little piece of land he'd bought. But mostly I wanted to see if Mary Faith Hammond was around and if she was really going to have a baby.

I didn't have any trouble finding her. When I'd hidden Flash and crawled into the pine cave, there she sat, chewing on a big bite of sandwich. "I seen you hiding in here watching us move in," she said with her mouth full.

"I wasn't hiding. I play here all the time."

She took another bite and rolled her eyes up to say she didn't believe me.

"Was that your brother with the basketball?" I asked, to get her talking.

"He made All-Star last year, going to be captain this. Name's Larry," she said, nodding.

"He's tall. You Hammonds come tall."

"We take after our mama," she said.

"I didn't see her."

"Nope." She shot me a look that dared me to ask anything else.

"Well, where is she?" I said.

"Dead."

I was quiet a minute, angry and embarrassed to have fallen into Mary Faith's trap. But I wasn't about to ask any more about it or say I was sorry. Mary Faith didn't sound sorry, herself.

"Well, that was your daddy, wasn't it?" I asked.

"Yeah." She looked away, as if she had no interest in talking about him.

I didn't either; it was her I meant to find out about.

I measured Mary Faith sitting there on the

ground, but it was hard to get an idea with her all folded up. She didn't look as thick as she should. "Are you going to have a baby?" I finally said right out.

Her head snapped back like she'd been slapped. "Where'd you hear that?"

"My aunt Map."

"She's a liar."

I giggled, thinking what Map would do if she heard herself called a liar. "No, she's not, she never lies," I said. "She says you're going to have a baby."

But Mary Faith wasn't going to talk about herself. "What's your name?" she asked.

"Prin."

"What kind of name is that?"

"Elizabeth."

"So who calls you Prin?"

"Everybody. It's my nickname," I said. I'd been laughed at before about being called Princess and wasn't about to tell Mary Faith Hammond it was what my daddy called me. I turned the talk right back toward her, quick. "You're Mary Faith Hammond and you go to Bartlett High like my sister, Jo Lynn. What grade are you in?"

"I'm not in a grade." Mary Faith patted her hair and stuck her chin up in the air. But the corners of her mouth were twitching. "Pregnant girls can't go to high school. You can tell your snotty sister I won't be back at Bartlett this fall."

"You won't?" I was so surprised, I couldn't help letting it show.

Mary Faith didn't answer, just kept on playing with her hair.

"Our mama's expecting, too," I stuttered, just to have something to say. "She can't teach next year either, till after the baby's born."

Mary Faith ran her tongue over her top teeth.

"And my daddy's in the hospital, might be there all the way to Christmas. Jo Lynn and me'll have to take care of Mama when she has the baby," I went on, my mind racing. "Who's going to take care of you?"

"I'll be in California by the time mine's due. My husband's in the Army out there, boot camp." She shot me a sideways look, her head tilted up and a hand wiping sweat off her throat. "I'm just living here until he can get an apartment on the base."

I tried to catch up with what she was saying. Jo Lynn hadn't even been out with a boy yet, and blushed and got stammer tongued when I asked her about them. And now Mary Faith Hammond was telling me she was expecting and already married!

I opened my mouth to ask how she could be married and only fifteen, but I'd waited too long.

"What're your horses' names?" She was looking through the pine branches at Red and Lady, who had come up to the fence nickering for Flash.

"The sorrel gelding's Big Red. He's my daddy's horse. The other two are mine."

"You think I could ride sometime?" Mary Faith asked, sounding shy. "I'd like to ride the big red one."

"Red won't let anybody but Daddy get near him."

"I bet he'd let me."

I snorted. "You can't ride Red. Even with a curb bit it takes a grown man to handle him."

She watched Red awhile, squinting into the sunlight. "How come he's so hard to handle if he's gelded?" she asked.

I frowned at her, my mind a blank.

"I thought it was only stallions that acted mean. Gelding makes him gentler, don't it? Ain't that why you gelded him?" She waited for an answer.

But I didn't have one, because I didn't know what she was asking. *Gelded* was just a horse word, one I'd never thought to ask Daddy about. All I knew was it wasn't a word for color, like sorrel and bay, but had to do with Red being male.

Mary Faith was giggling, both hands clamped over her mouth, her eyes making fun of me above the bits of red polish left on her fingernails. "You don't even know what gelding is," she snickered, glad to have me on the spot like I'd had her not two minutes before.

"I do too," I said.

"Then tell me."

I blushed.

"It means he's been *fixed*," she shouted, clapping her hands. "He can't make baby horses!"

"Foals," I shouted back. "He can't make *foals* and I knew that. And you don't even know the word for baby horses!"

But she was laughing too hard to hear. I scrambled out of the cave backward and went straight home, mad enough to cry.

That night I looked up *fix* and *geld* in Jo Lynn's dictionary. *Fix* was what I thought it was, "securely place or fasten." *Geld* meant "to castrate." *Castrate* just said "to emasculate; to geld," and *emasculate* said "to castrate; to geld."

I gave up. The dictionary talked just like Mama and Aunt Map and Jo Lynn when it came to sex things. But I decided if Mary Faith and I ever visited again, I was going to ask her straight out why

Red couldn't make babies. And while I was at it, I was going to ask her if she was really married.

In fact, I might ask her about a lot of things, the kind that nobody in my house would talk about. Mary Faith Hammond seemed to *know* stuff, and if I treated her nice and asked just right, maybe she'd tell me.

IT WAS TWO more days before I finally saw Mr. Mose Hardy. I rode Flash around Otwell's Lakes, and when I got back, a pickup truck was parked at the top of the hill. I rode over to the fence and there he was.

Mr. Mose was tall and thin, with pepper-white hair. His hands were hard, like Daddy's, with knuckles that looked like hollowed-out pools of hide.

All down our fence line he had unrolled chicken wire on his side of the posts. On the other side of his property fence posts were lying on the ground in a pile, with more rolls of chicken wire.

"How's your daddy getting on in the hospital, Miss Prin?" he called when I rode up.

"Just fine," I answered, surprised he remembered my name.

"That's good. He's always bragging about what

a fine rider you are, how you help him around the place."

"Yes, sir, I do," I said, shy and proud. Just hearing about Daddy made me miss him more.

"What are you putting that kind of fence up for?" I said after a minute.

"For Joe Leonard."

"Who's Joe Leonard?"

He didn't seem to hear, concentrating on tying strings across in a straight line between sticks he was nailing in the ground.

"What are you building?" I said, louder.

"A house."

"Seems mighty narrow."

"Big enough. All me and Joe Leonard need."

"I sometimes want to visit the Otwells' horses," I said. "I cut through the fence right here and go across the pasture."

Mr. Mose looked over the fence he had rolled out, then down at the road, measuring things with his eye.

"What I'll do is I'll put some little boards up this post, like steps, that you can climb up and over on when you want to."

"All right."

Flash had her head swung around looking over her shoulder, and when I looked back, a man was walking down the drive to our house. "I have to go," I said, turning Flash toward the barn.

Mr. Mose was looking, too. "B.Z. Hammond's coming to call," he said. He spit. "Well, it is Sunday."

BY THE TIME I got to the house, Mary Faith's daddy was sitting with Mama and Map on the screened porch. Mama sat on the edge of her chair, feet flat on the floor, ankles and knees together. When her hands weren't waving around talking, she folded them together in her lap around a white handkerchief. She was sitting Sunday, and so was Aunt Map, who had pulled her chair close to Mama's like she needed protection. Neither one of them had a welcome face on.

Jo Lynn was just going into the house, dressed in a fresh skirt and blouse, her hair put over to the side with a new barrette like she was expecting company.

"Prin," Mama said, her voice rising at the end of my name. She didn't look at me but held out her hand, palm up with the fingers flicking back toward her, meaning come on in.

"Mr. Hammond, this is my younger daughter, Elizabeth. This is Mr. B.Z. Hammond, Prin, who's moved into the old Thompson place."

Mr. B.Z. was getting to his feet, holding himself up on the arm of a wicker chair that tilted; he tilted, too, like he wasn't heavy enough to stay upright. Red veins threaded his cheeks and the end of his nose, and his eyes drifted around the screened porch like he was too shy to look anybody in the eye. He wore a bow tie and a short-sleeved white shirt that needed cleaning and ironing. The toes of his shoes were as scuffed as mine. Up close he was smaller than I thought, and he smelled, a strong, sour man smell that Daddy's truck drivers had at the end of the day.

"I'm pleased to meet you, Elizabeth," he said.

I jumped. I should have spoken first, but I'd lost my place studying him. "Hi," I said, then, "How do you do," because Mama frowned at me over his shoulder.

"Go help Jo Lynn with the tea, dear," she said.

There wasn't anyplace I could hide and listen, so I went on into the kitchen. Jo Lynn already had the ice in glasses. "Of all people," she said, running over to the old painted cabinet where Mama kept the napkins. "Why did Mary Faith Hammond have to move in next door? Now she'll expect me to be friends."

"I think she's neat," I said, and walked over to

the big window to watch Mr. B.Z., Mama, and Aunt Map talking.

"What do you know about anything! Come open the door, silly," Jo Lynn hissed, careful with the tray of tall tea glasses. I opened the screen porch door for her, too, so I could stay and listen.

"How's Mr. Campbell getting on?" Mr. B.Z. was asking.

"He's doing fine," Mama said. "Slow, though. It'll be a while."

"I'd be proud to offer my help if you need something done around the place while he's gone."

A warning passed between Mama and Aunt Map, with Mama looking right at Mr. Hammond and saying, "That's kind of you, Mr. Hammond, but I believe we can manage."

"I do respect a proud woman, Mrs. Campbell." Mr. B.Z. nodded, his gap-toothed smile swinging between Mama and Map. "But it seems to me a woman needs a man around to keep a place up, 'specially a place as big and nice as this. You find yourself short on help, you jest give me a holler."

"I'll keep that in mind." Mama's voice was the same cold one she used to one of Daddy's truck drivers who came to the house drunk and wanted to borrow money.

Mr. B.Z. didn't seem to notice, but smiled at Jo Lynn over the glass of tea she was handing him. "I believe you're in my daughter's class," he said.

Jo Lynn drew back, then said, "No, sir, Mary Faith's a year behind me."

"That's because she's had to repeat a grade," Mr. B.Z. said right out. He sighed. "You have two fine girls, Mrs. Campbell. They're real pretty young ladies."

Mama's shoulders stiffened, and Aunt Map leaned forward in her chair.

He went on. "A girl needs a mama—it takes a woman's touch to make a lady. I don't think Mary Faith's going to amount to much; I can't seem to do nothing with her." He slanted his sad eyes at Mama and Aunt Map. "Mrs. Hammond's been gone now for five years, and I miss her ever' day."

Map pressed back in her chair, Mama looked at a loss for words until Mr. B.Z. said something about fence lines, and they all moved away from the edge of something uneasy. Finally Mr. Hammond stood up and tilted himself forward from the waist three times, a little bow to every one of them. He gave me a smile that from anybody else wouldn't have made me feel strange.

"Well, I never thought he'd have the nerve to

come calling, and I don't like it one little bit that he did," Map exploded when he was out of sight. She leaned forward, her hand on Mama's arm. "And offering to help out like we were supposed to jump all over ourselves thanking him! I wouldn't have that man around my place if I'd lost one arm and both legs. Why the things I've heard—"

Mama's look stopped Map from saying whatever she was going to. I was about to ask what she'd heard when Jo Lynn started dancing around on one foot, watching a car come down the driveway. "Mama-a-a," she whined.

Aunt Map gathered up the tea glasses, her lips set tight on a statement she could barely hold. Mama sat until Goose Jamison came in and said hello. Then she excused herself and pushed me along ahead of her toward the house. "They don't need you watching," she said.

"Mr. B.Z. smells," I said, fishing for whatever they would tell me. "Is that why you didn't ask him in the living room?"

"The living room's all torn up for painting. You know that." Mama shrugged.

But Aunt Map smiled at me like I'd hit close to something. "Precocious child," she said. "Sometimes I think there's hope for you."

"You just forget about the Hammonds," Mama added, tucking hair into my braid. "We won't be seeing any more of them."

MAP DROVE OFF, and Mama went to her room to take a nap before going to see Daddy. I looked around Jo Lynn's bedroom, but she hadn't left anything interesting out. From her windows I could see her and Goose, black cutout shapes against the sunlight, their heads bending together and apart, Jo Lynn talking bright and loud.

They seemed more interested in each other than married people like Mama and Daddy, who were real toward each other and didn't pretend they were happy all the time. I thought how Mr. B.Z. had acted toward Mama the same way Jo Lynn was acting with Goose now, like he wanted to look brighter and better than he was.

Thinking about all that, I cut through the bathroom and out the back door, looking for something to do. I banged on an old woodpile awhile, but nothing slid out, only some roaches across the top boards. Then I went over to the water trough to see if there were any slugs I could put salt on.

Banging on woodpiles and salting slugs was how I expected the whole summer to be before the Hammonds moved in. But having them as neighbors was changing everything. Already there were feelings and thoughts flying around our house that had never been there before and nobody wanted to put a name to. Jo Lynn and Map were upset, and Mama was trying to act like nothing had happened at all.

I wasn't going along with Mama on that. There was something different about the Hammonds, and it seemed like everybody but me had some idea what it was.

Now the summer looked good for two things. The first would be to help Mr. Mose build his house and learn how it was done. But better than that, I could keep an eye on the Hammonds and find out what it was about them that nobody seemed to want me to know.

Four

I CRAWLED INTO the pine cave whenever I could to spy on our new neighbors, but the Hammonds kept their shades pulled down, and their driveway was nearly always empty. The only change that showed somebody lived next door was in the yard, where a basketball hoop went up outside the kitchen door and a bare patch of ground began stretching out through the shaggy grass underneath it.

Then I realized that every day the shade on the Hammonds' kitchen door was at a different level

and had a handkerchief or a fork or spoon tied to
its pull string, like somebody inside was sending
a signal. I felt a little embarrassed, knowing that
Mary Faith was watching me watch her house.

One day when she signaled, though, it was different. I was riding back from Otwell's Lakes when
she called my name. I tied Flash to the fence and
crawled into the pine cave, where she was lying
doubled up on the thick mattress of pine needles
holding her stomach. "I got a stomachache real
bad," she said. "I done lost everything I ate this
morning, and I think I got a fever."

I crouched under the pine branches and stared
at her, wondering why she was in my cave instead of home in bed. After a while she flattened
out on her back, breathing through pursed-up lips
and pressing the tips of her fingers down on her
stomach.

"Don't you need to tell your daddy, maybe have
him take you to the doctor?" I said, alarmed at the
sweat breaking out on her white face.

She blew her breath out three or four times. "I
don't have a doctor. If we're really sick, we go to
the free clinic down at Methodist Hospital."

"Well don't you need to go there now?"

"Nobody's home to take me."

I knew what she was asking. "Wait right here,"

I said, already backing out of the cave. "I'll go get Mama."

She just groaned.

I found Mama tending to truck business in Daddy's office. "Mary Faith Hammond's lying up in the pines on our place, and she's sick. I think she needs to go to the doctor. You better come quick," I said, breathless from running all the way home.

Mama's hand stopped with the telephone receiver halfway to her ear. "Can't her daddy take her?"

"No, ma'am, he's not home," I said. "Please come see. She looks like she's feeling real bad."

Mama put the receiver down, rubbed her face with both hands, and sighed. "All right, I'll walk up there with you and see what's going on."

But before we got up to the pine cave, Mr. B.Z.'s old truck wheezed into the Hammonds' back yard. Mama cut across to the old iron gate and called to him.

"I believe your girl's not feeling well, Mr. Hammond. Maybe you ought to take her to see the doctor."

"Mrs. Campbell." Mr. Hammond tipped his cap and turned a puzzled look toward his house.

"Prin, you go tell Mary Faith her father's home to take care of her," Mama said. "She's up here in our pines, Mr. Hammond, waiting for Prin to come by, I expect, so she could ask for help."

"I'm sorry she's been a trouble to you. Sometimes she gits sick of a morning, but it usually wears right off. There probably ain't no call for the doctor."

I saw a mean look on Mr. Hammond's face before I ran off to the pines for Mary Faith. She was already trying to crawl out of the cave, crying a little and too sick to stand without leaning some of her weight on me.

"He's going to be mad at me," she whispered, looking scared. "He's gonna think I got sick jest to spite him."

"How can he think that?" I whispered back. "Anybody can see you're not putting on."

"Looks to me like a doctor is just what she does need," Mama was saying, coming to help Mary Faith through the gate. "Dr. Emerson is our doctor, and he's right there in Raleigh Springs. I'll call ahead if you like."

"We done troubled you enough, Mrs. Campbell," Mr. B.Z. said, helping Mary Faith get in the truck. "I reckon we'll go on down to the clinic at Methodist in case it's more than just morning sickness."

Mama turned away, but I hung on the iron gate

watching them drive off, and was still watching through the back window when Mr. B.Z.'s palm came up and slapped across the top of Mary Faith's head.

My head smarted like I'd been hit myself, I was so surprised.

"Mama, Mr. B.Z.—"

"I'd just as soon not get mixed up in the Hammonds' affairs," she called back. "You did right, offering help if Mary Faith needed it, but it's her daddy's responsibility to take care of her, not ours."

"But he—"

"Don't forget to bring Flash home."

"Yes, ma'am," I mumbled, scrambling over the pasture fence.

I couldn't understand why Mr. B.Z. hit Mary Faith just because she was sick. Then I remembered what Map had said about him, and I shivered. If Mr. B.Z. used to hit his wife, why would he think a thing of hitting his daughter?

I CHECKED THE cave every day for Mary Faith. Finally I found her inside, using a board as a lap desk and drawing pictures of Red by holding a pencil sideways between her thumb and other fingers. I was glad to see her.

"You all right?" I asked, because she still looked a little pale.

She nodded, concentrating on her drawing. "I had a touch of flu is all. And the morning sickness. The doctor says to eat better, get plenty of rest, and I'll be fine."

"What's morning sickness?" I asked.

My trying to help her when she was feeling bad must have made a difference, because she didn't make fun of me now. "Morning sickness is what women have when they first get pregnant. With their bodies changing to grow the baby, it's hard to get up and get going in the mornings. You're kind of sick to your stomach. It don't amount to much."

She squinted at her drawing, then turned it around and showed it to me without my asking. The sketch of Big Red was unfinished, but it was him exactly, standing sideways with his head swung around like he was looking out of the picture right at me.

But what was more interesting was the sketch of me right beside it. I hadn't known she was doing that.

"You're good," I said, meaning it. "You got Red exact, and just about got me right."

"I'll get you perfect next time." She grinned,

pleased that I liked her drawing. "I just need to study you a little more."

She put the drawings to the side and pulled a wrinkled grocery sack into her lap.

"What's in there?" I asked.

"Makeup."

"Sure is a lot of it."

"I asked Mr. Landis at the drugstore for all his samples and old stuff." She dumped the makeup out in a swept-clean place between her legs. "You want me to make you up?" she asked, looking at her own face in a cracked hand mirror. There was a magnifying mirror on my side, and one of my huge gray eyes flashed in and out of the mirror as Mary Faith moved it around.

"Sure," I said, shrugging, not because I wanted to be made up but because I wanted to talk to her.

She was rubbing pancake makeup on my cheeks with the ends of her fingers before I thought of anything to say, though. "What *does* geld mean?" I said.

She almost laughed, then caught herself.

"I tried to look it up," I said, when she didn't answer. "It said to castrate, but I don't know what that means, either."

This time she did laugh, a loud, open laugh that had no teasing in it. "You ought to ask your mama about things like that," she said, getting out some lipstick.

"She wouldn't tell me," I said, trying to hold my lips tight and still. "But she likes me to learn new words, and I already know that one, I just don't know what it means."

Mary Faith sat back on her heels and studied my face for half a minute, then rummaged around in the makeup before she answered. "It's how they cut a male horse or cow to make them not able to make babies. You know." She wet the end of an eyebrow pencil in her mouth while making a scissoring motion with one hand.

"I *don't* know," I said. "Cut how? What's there to cut? Red doesn't have a mark on him."

This time a giggle exploded out of Mary Faith, spraying spit all over the cave. She was red in the face and had a hard time getting words out. "Balls. They cut their balls off, their testicles."

My own face turned to fire. I dropped my head to my knees and began giggling too, thinking of Red's thing that sometimes swung like a thick limp rope from between his back legs. *Testicles* was something he would have had back there, too; it was the man's sex part that made the sperm that came out of the penis and got inside a woman to fertilize her eggs and make a baby. I knew *testicles* because of the book Mama kept in the back linen closet, top shelf, a book she shared with Jo Lynn. I got it out of where I saw Jo Lynn sneaking it back one day.

I rolled around blushing and giggling, thinking how I'd been right about Mary Faith. She *did* know things, and she'd just told me something nobody in my own family would have ever said. When I caught my breath, I gave her a big, grateful grin, letting her know I was ready to be friends.

All of a sudden I didn't want to ask her another question I had: Was she really married? Acting like I didn't believe what she said wasn't friendly.

"If you want to come over to Otwell's Lakes tomorrow afternoon, I'll teach you to ride Flash" is what I said.

But she finished drawing on my eyebrows before she answered, sounding a little sad. "The doctor says I shouldn't do anything rough—I might lose the baby."

"Riding isn't rough unless you gallop."

"I don't want to take no chances." She hesitated, then added almost in a whisper, "I shouldn't want this baby, but I do. I want somebody that I can take care of, somebody that's mine. I get real lonesome sometimes."

So I got an answer to my question without even

asking it: she wasn't married. If she had been, she would already have had somebody that was hers, somebody to take care of.

"I get lonesome sometimes, too," I said, feeling a little sorry for her. "Maybe you and me can do stuff together until the baby comes."

"Maybe," she said, already looking sorry she'd said so much. She was quiet while she unbraided my hair and pinned it on top of my head. Then she held the mirror up, right side to me, so I could see what she'd done.

Seeing my own face looking so grown-up felt strange. My gray eyes looked almost blue, my teeth looked small and white next to the lipstick, and my hair was a mess of dark curls that wouldn't stay pinned up.

I looked older, but still ordinary, not different and interesting like Mary Faith. "Draw those lines around my eyes like an Egyptian lady," I asked, and she did.

Then I looked like she had the first time I saw her, except I didn't have a black eye under the makeup.

"You're going to be as pretty as Jo Lynn," Mary Faith said.

"Mama says I look like Daddy."

"What's he like?"

"We go riding together all the time. He laughs a lot and would never give me a black eye, even when he's real mad."

That about the black eye just popped out, and right away I knew I'd said the wrong thing. Mary Faith stiffened, then started gathering up her makeup and drawing tablet.

"Aren't you going to make yourself up?" I asked, trying to change the subject.

"I already know how I look."

"Well, why don't you draw me with makeup on?" But she kept on backing out of the cave, her head down so I could see that the roots of her hair weren't the same yellow color as the rest.

I RODE BACK to Otwell's Lakes and tried to wash up, squinting at my reflection in the water and thinking how Daddy would laugh if he saw the black lines stretching from the corners of my eyes, or how my hair was falling out of Mary Faith's bobby pins.

Then another reflection seemed to ripple across the water and I saw Mr. B.Z.'s palm slapping up against Mary Faith's head. All the good feelings I'd had talking to her melted away, and I felt uneasy. For a minute I thought maybe I would act like Mama and pretend the Hammonds didn't live next door.

But right away I decided not to; after all, Mary Faith was just a girl, and needed a friend even if she was pregnant and not married. And there wasn't any reason I'd ever have to have anything to do with her daddy.

Five

I MISSED MY daddy a lot. Every Sunday I sent him
a letter telling about the horses and what I was
doing, and Mama brought one back from him. But
that wasn't like talking to him. We used to talk
about everything from horses to Zane Grey to
baseball, and when I ran across something I didn't
understand, Daddy would tell me. I wished our
letters could fill up the long empty afternoons
when Daddy should have been riding with me, or
teaching me how to jump Lady over the low

hurdles he'd put up behind the barn, but they didn't.

Daddy left a big empty space in his garden, in the barn, where I had to struggle to get my saddle off its high rack, and in our yard, where the grass was growing as high as my knees right up by the front door. I missed him in the living room, too, where just Mama and Jo Lynn and me read at night, or in the hall, where I never bumped into him coming out their bedroom door.

Map started sitting at his place at the table every Wednesday night and Sunday afternoon while Mama went to the hospital. It was on one of those hot June Sundays that Mr. B.Z. came by again. Outside there wasn't a sound, and inside only the roar of the fan down the bedroom hall, and me sloshing dishwater around. A fly buzzed around the window over the sink, and two wasps, brown and doubled up dead, lay on the sill.

From where I was clearing our plates from the dinner table, I could look over to the living room at Mama lying on the sofa.

"I've just about finished the jobs Brian had contracted for," she was telling Map. "I haven't found any other work, though."

"Sell those trucks," Map said. "And the horses

and a piece of land to Mose Hardy. He'll be glad to have it and you'll never miss it."

"Lock down and quit living, you mean," Mama said. "I think there's something between here and there, don't you?" Her voice would have stopped anybody but Map.

"You've got to get some money coming in, Ada Ruth," she argued.

"Don't tell me what I already know, Margaret Ann. If you've got any bright ideas about how to do that, then I'll be happy to listen," Mama snapped back.

For a minute there was total quiet, Mama and Map looking off to opposite corners of the room.

Then Map said, gentler but still meaning it, "Ada Ruth, you're worrying yourself to death with those trucks. You've got to let go before you make yourself sick. You look awful."

What Map said was true, even if it was mean. With the baby growing fatter in her stomach, Mama's face had become white and tired-looking, and blue veins had popped out on her legs so she had to lie down with her feet propped up higher than her head. She had begun to move slower, too, like a stiff Tinkertoy woman with a round middle and stick arms and legs.

I was staring at Mama, thinking how much she had changed, when Mr. B.Z. Hammond's voice snapped all our heads around and dropped Mama's feet to the floor.

"Anybody to home?" he yelled from our front yard.

Mama and Map looked wide-eyed at each other for half a minute before Mama headed toward the door.

Seeing Mr. B.Z. again made me feel funny, but I didn't want to miss anything. I stood just behind Mama, where I could see Mr. B.Z. and his old lawn mower that was half buried in the grass of our side yard.

He had on rumpled khaki work pants and a scoop-necked, sleeveless undershirt that let the hairs on his chest and under his arms stick out. He didn't tip his cap when Mama came to the door.

"We're home, Mr. Hammond. What can we do for you?" Mama stood with one hand on the screen door, the other sneaking up to fasten the hook.

"Not a thing, Mrs. Ada. It's what I can do for you that brung me. Thought I'd cut your grass right here around the house, sort of to say thank you for being so nice to my Mary Faith when she was putting on sick the other day."

"That isn't necessary, Mr. Hammond. We really didn't do anything," Mama said.

"You had kind thoughts, and that's enough to need repaying. I'll just clip a little around the steps, too, sort of clean out so snakes and all won't get too close to the front door here."

Mr. B.Z. smiled for no reason while he talked, and spit shot through the gap between his front teeth. He never looked right at Mama, but shifted his eyes across the front of our house like he was memorizing it.

Mama cleared her throat. "This is Sunday, Mr. Hammond, a day of rest. We don't work on the Lord's day in this household."

I looked at Mama sideways, knowing Daddy cut the grass on Sundays.

"And I'm asking Brian's Sunday school class to cut our grass, thank you just the same. I don't believe there's any call for you to bother yourself about doing for us."

Mr. Hammond looked stumped, half bent over the sidewalk with his clippers open over a stalk of tall grass. Then his lips split open in a smile while the clippers smacked shut around the grass. "I'll

clip just a little then, Mrs. Ada, so's I can say thank
you without getting the Lord too mad at me. Maybe
we'll come out just about even."

Mr. B.Z. began clipping the tall grass like Mama
hadn't just told him not to. There wasn't a thing
she could do about it.

She sat back down on the sofa, stiff and proper,
and for a long, tense time the only sound in the
whole world seemed to be Mr. B.Z.'s clippers
snipping up the walk toward our front door. He
snipped around Mama's rosebushes close to the
porch; then gradually the sound of his clippers
moved away from the latched screen.

There wasn't any conversation until he'd quit
altogether and called out a cheery, "I'll be going
now," and the dragging sound of his old lawn-
mower died away up our drive.

"Well, I never," Map breathed. "The nerve of
that man! How'd he get all the way down here
without our hearing him?"

"We couldn't hear over the fan, I guess," Mama
said, fanning a hand in front of her face to give
herself more air.

I squeezed out the dishrag and walked back to
the table to brush up crumbs. I was hoping she'd
talk about him when she got her breath back.

Instead, she called to me, "Are you finished with the dishes?"

"No, ma'am."

"Leave them and go play—you can finish when it's cooler."

I tried hiding around the hall corner so I could eavesdrop, but Mama must have seen me, because she told me again to go play outside.

I climbed a sweetgum tree and swung over to the roof of the old garage, a place I like to go to be alone and think.

Mr. B.Z. had acted like Mama hadn't told him to leave us alone, and Mama and Map had been real uncomfortable with him right outside our door. Mama was more at ease around Daddy's truck drivers, who smelled sweaty and used bad grammar like Mr. B.Z. but didn't make you feel like something was going on behind their eyes that you wouldn't want to know about.

That's all the thinking I could do. It was warm on the roof, a little breezy, with nice noises from the leaves, and I fell asleep.

When I woke up, it was late afternoon. There was a full ghost moon in the east and the sun was just below the trees to the west, so when it got good dark, the night would be just right for rid-

ing. I hadn't been since the Hammonds had moved
in.

I sleep with my head at the foot of the top bunk
so I can see the moon, and the horses when they
run. From there I can reach over to the windowsill
and undo the two hooks at the bottom of the screen
and swing it out. If I lean out the window sideways, I can catch a limb of a pin oak and skinny
down.

Even on a bright night, I have to be careful
around the horses. They spook easy. I've learned
never to run toward Red or surprise him in the
moondark. So when I slipped out that night, I
walked across the pasture easy and slow, talking
low all the time. The horses were in a quiet drowsy
bunch in the valley, and so used to me they didn't
move. Even Red stayed close enough to touch.

I swung up on Flash and sat for a few minutes,
letting her wake up and get used to my being there.
Over at the Hammonds' I heard the sound of a car
shutting off, then a door banging like somebody
had just got home. I was a little uneasy about riding over to find out what was going on; I sure
didn't want to see Mr. B.Z. But it was dark enough
so nobody would spot me in the pine cave even if
they knew to look. So I pulled on Flash's mane

and kicked her with my bare heels, and after a while we were over by the Hammonds' fence, where yellow sparks of light were shining through the pines. There was a smothered sound, too, a thudding like a ball being thrown up against the house.

That's what it was. From the cave I saw Larry Hammond throwing the basketball one-armed as hard as he could against the screen door to the kitchen. The doorframe shivered and clapped against the house every time the ball hit it. The top half of the screen ripped, a windowpane shattered into the house, with a few quick sparkles of glass flying out into the yard. I saw it break but didn't hear it, because Larry Hammond was screaming. "You lay a hand on her and I'll kill you, you bastard," he yelled, running up the steps and tearing at the doorframe with his bare hands. "I swear to God I'll break your head open if you so much as touch her again." I heard him plain, but he was saying things I didn't really understand. He was mad, and I huddled against a pine trunk to make sure he couldn't see me.

I heard other screams, too, through the shattered window, and noises, like things were being thrown around inside the house. Larry Hammond had his arm stuck through the broken window, trying to get to the inside doorknob. All of a sudden the kitchen door was yanked open about a foot, slammed shut, yanked open again. Mary Faith came pitching out through what was left of the screen door, knocking Larry backward. He landed on his back, and she landed heavy and stomach down on top of his foot. I heard her head hit the ground.

The shade at the kitchen door was pulled open, spilling a sharp yellow square of light on the ground, and Mr. B.Z. Hammond stuck his face against the top pane of glass. "You want that slut?" he screamed, his face twisted and hateful. "Well, take her and get out of here before I beat the hell outa you both."

Then the shade was yanked shut and the kitchen lights snapped off, leaving just moondark, clean and sharp. There wasn't any noise except the ordinary drumming of bullfrogs from around the lake and the quiet rasp of crickets rubbing their legs together, and the strange thumping of my heart.

I felt it moving things around inside my chest. I couldn't breathe. I looked at the barbed wire stretched tight between me and the Hammonds. Even though they were on the other side, what was going on scared me to death. I wished I was safe in my own bed and hadn't gone night riding. I wished I knew what to do about Mary Faith and her brother lying there like they were dead.

After a while Larry pulled his foot out from under Mary Faith and sat up. He put an arm around her, helped her straighten out her nightgown, and let her cry against his shoulder. "Are you all right?" he said over and over. "Did he hurt you?" But she just cried and held her stomach where she had landed on his foot. Finally he got her on her feet, and leaning against each other, they made it around the corner of the house, got in his car, and drove off.

I had to get home. I busted out of the cave too fast, scaring Flash and Big Red and Lady, who were grazing next to the fence. They snorted and jumped back and we all took off running, them across the pasture and me down the driveway. I didn't even feel the gravel, but ran as hard as I could.

I cut across the mimosa patch and climbed the pin oak, skinning my leg bad, got inside, and hooked the screen. I was shaking and breathing so hard, so hard! Grit and trash were stuck all over me, which I dusted off on the wall side of the bed. I rolled up in my sheet and put my head under the pillow.

Mama heard me crying. I felt her hand on me. She pulled the pillow off my head and said, "Prin? What's the matter, Prin?" and I cried while she rubbed my head, hot and wet around the hairline, and she said, "Hush now, I'm here, it's all right. It's just a dream."

Six

IT WASN'T A dream. The next morning my legs had horsehair and sweat on them, and my scratched knee had bled on the sheets. I hadn't dreamed a thing.

I had never wanted to talk to Daddy so bad; I needed to tell him about Mr. B.Z. But I couldn't get to him, so Mama was my only choice for talking. I had to tell her what had happened, even if she was going to be mad about my night riding. But right after breakfast Mama fainted.

I yelled; Jo Lynn ran in from the clothesline and sat on the floor crying and trying to help Mama up. I didn't stop to think, just took off running all the way across our pasture to Mr. Mose's place and told him my mama was sick and would he please come.

Before we got to the front door, I was embarrassed I'd called him. It should have been a woman going into Mama's bedroom and helping her up off the floor. But Mr. Mose did it, and Mama let him, clutching her house robe tight across her chest and not one time looking in his face.

Mr. Mose didn't look at her, either, when he swung her feet up on the bed and pulled the sheet up. Then he stepped out to the hall and closed the door before asking Jo Lynn who our doctor was.

"Dr. Emerson," she whispered.

"You go call him," he wheezed, like he'd run and not driven all the way to our house. "You tell him Mose Hardy says to get hisself out here right now, and bring his nurse. Miss Ada needs attention."

Jo Lynn went back to stay with Mama, and Mr. Mose and me sat at the kitchen table drinking iced tea and not talking until Dr. Emerson and his nurse got there.

Dr. Emerson said Mama wasn't really sick, but

needed to rest and take better care of herself or she might lose the baby. "I believe Miss Margaret Ann's your only relative?" he asked Jo Lynn with his eyebrows up, and right away I knew who I should have called.

While Jo Lynn was telephoning Map, I went back to the bedroom and pushed Mama's door open to where I could see her lying in bed piled around with pillows. She was staring at the ceiling and crying with no sound. She cut her eyes over at me without moving her head.

"Did I give you a scare?" she asked, turning her hand palm up on the sheet.

"Yes, ma'am," I said, going in and taking her hand. It was cold. "Are you all right?"

"Of course," she said, but her voice was little. "It's just a faint, the second one in my whole life. I felt it coming." She squeezed my hand.

"Have you still got the baby?"

"Yes, I've got the baby. I'm going to have this baby, a little brother or sister for you."

"What if it makes you sick?"

"It won't." Mama squeezed my hand harder. "Don't you worry about that. It'll just make me have to stay in bed a lot, rest, so I can carry it till it's big enough to be born. That's all."

Mama's room was still morning cool, shaded by
the old cedar outside the window. The gauze curtains lifted with the breeze. On Daddy's dresser
the clock was ticking. Everything was like it was
any morning, except for Mama lying there in
bed.

"We don't need Map," I said. "I'll bring you
sandwiches. Jo Lynn and me can do everything till
you feel better."

She almost smiled. "I wish you were right, but
I expect Map'll be right handy to have around. She
won't be here but a couple of weeks—just till I'm
on my feet again."

I thought a minute, remembering what I'd been
on my way to tell her when she fainted and wishing I still could. But now that wouldn't be right—
she wasn't well, and already had enough to worry
about.

Then I had a new thought. "What about seeing
Daddy? Who's going to go see him? Can I?" I
asked, hoping maybe I could tell him after all.

"You know you can't. I can still go to the hospital, Prin; I'm not sick-sick. I just have to rest a
lot and be careful about the baby."

Mama's fingers were getting warmer.

"When'll he come home?"

"Probably in September, about the time the baby's due."

September seemed as far away as Daddy was. I didn't have anybody to talk to about the Hammonds, at least until Mama got well again.

"Okay." I looked at the books she had stacked on her bed table. "You want to read a Zane Grey? I've got a good one."

"No, I want to sleep. Dr. Emerson gave me some pills, and they're working. You run along now and tell Mr. Mose and the doctor thank you. And don't worry, Prin—we'll be all right."

"Yes, ma'am."

Mama latched her fingers together across her belly and closed her eyes. I left the door cracked and went back to the living room, but Dr. Emerson and his nurse were already pulling away in his big white car, and Mr. Mose was halfway back home.

MAP STAYED OVER that night, and the next morning, while Mama was at her baby doctor and Jo Lynn was at baton practice, she and I followed a big truck packed with her things to our house. Some men moved her bed into the room Daddy had built for an office, while Map and me carried in little things—plaster praying hands, a glass table lamp with a pink shade and a satin bow, and a silver-framed picture of my dead uncle Albert that had water-colored brown hair and lips that were almost orange.

Map hung her dresses with an inch between them in her chifforobe and lined her shoes up on the floor, then opened the door to the new bathroom Daddy had added on for himself. There wasn't anyplace in the bathroom to put things except for a ledge at the back of the sink with a hollowed-out place for soap.

"What am I supposed to do with all these?" she asked me, pointing to the things in her overnight case. "Why didn't you put shelves in this bathroom? There's not even a hamper for dirty clothes."

"It's supposed to be just for men."

"I'll have to get me something. This isn't civilized." She put on a straw hat and gloves and left without saying a word about me going with her. Mama wasn't going to like me being home alone even in daylight, but I didn't mind—there were some things I wanted to do.

I went to Jo Lynn's room that she always kept the doors shut to and tried on her red satin majorette suit and white boots. I put on some perfume and lipstick and went to the hall mirror that showed me full length. I didn't like me. My legs looked skinny, and the suit top had empty pointy places for where Jo Lynn was growing breasts. My friend Sarah Chaney says girls grow things on top, boys on bottom. But boys are born with things on bottom; I saw Mrs. Honeycutt changing her baby's diaper in the church nursery and he already had it.

I put the suit back in the closet and looked at Jo Lynn's Bartlett High notebook. Boys' names were written all over the cover, some inside hearts shot through with arrows. I counted, but nobody was named more times than anybody else. But inside was a list, "Jo Lynn Campbell's Fabulous Summer Frolic," with twenty-five names, fifteen boys and ten girls.

An end-of-summer party is one of a whole list of things Jo Lynn wanted for the good and special thing Mama had promised. Others were buying a dress at Goldsmith's, going on a date, getting a permanent, and going to majorette camp down at Mississippi State University. She wanted me to trade her my wish so she could do two things, but she didn't have anything I wanted.

"I want to invite everybody at church and everybody at Bartlett to my party," she'd said at lunch the other day. "I want to have it on the screen porch, and I want everybody to bring their records, and have Coca-Cola and popcorn and cake, and paper streamers and play some games."

"Do you have a guest list? How many people are we talking about?" Mama said.

"There's more. I want you and Map to stay in the house. And I want Prin gone somewhere spending the night."

Mama's eyebrows went up. "I think I can keep Prin out of the way," she said. "You have a date picked out?"

"The first week of August."

"Jo Lynn wants to invite Dwight Chaney," I said, taking a bite of sandwich and watching her from the corner of my eye. "She's got a crush on Dwight."

"I do not."

"She watches him all the time in church."

"I do not."

"Flirts with him at choir practice."

"Well, you keep on the way you're going, no boy's ever going to look at you."

"All right by me," I said. "I bet you kiss back there in the choir room."

"We do not!"

"I bet you wished he would."

"Mama!"

"That's enough, Prin. Dwight's a nice boy."

"Got pimples. Bad breath."

"How do you know, smart aleck?" Jo Lynn said.

"Sarah told me. She says her mama makes him eat prunes to go to the bathroom."

"Prin!"

" 'S what she says."

"Nobody should have little sisters," Jo Lynn said, almost crying. I grinned at her, having so much fun I forgot when to quit.

"Says Dwight has a crush on Mary Faith Hammond."

As soon as I mentioned Mary Faith, I wished I hadn't. Mama and Jo Lynn were suddenly acting like I wasn't even there. Nobody said anything.

"Says she's a good lay," I went on, not able to stop myself.

"That's enough!" Mama snapped.

Jo Lynn stared at her plate.

I stared at mine too, knowing I was in trouble. I should have found out what a good lay was before I said it.

Mama slapped her knife down on her plate and

said, "Jo Lynn, you go start the ironing. Prin can do the dishes." That meant she wanted to talk to me by myself.

"I'll not have talk like that in this house," she told me. "If that's the kind of thing you hear at Sarah Chaney's, then maybe she shouldn't be your friend."

"You give us castor oil to go to the bathroom," I said, like I didn't know where she was heading. "What's so bad about talking about prunes?"

"Bathroom talk has no place in a lady's conversation. Neither does repeating ugly things about a neighbor." She looked at me hard, with a frown that meant she wasn't going to let me get away with anything. "You do the dishes and go straight to your room. And you stay there until you can figure out what a lady says and what she doesn't!"

"I'm sorry. I didn't mean to say anything bad about Mary Faith," I whispered, which was the truth. I hadn't meant to say her name at all.

OF COURSE MARY Faith's name was not on Jo Lynn's party list. But Larry Hammond's was, with a big red question mark right beside it. Larry Hammond was good-looking, and he was basketball captain, but I didn't see how Jo Lynn could think about asking him to her party if she wasn't going to ask Mary Faith.

I put Jo Lynn's notebook up and tried to find something else to do, something that would get my mind off Mary Faith. Across the pasture I could hear hammering at Mr. Mose's. Knowing he was there made me feel better, and for a second I thought of telling him about what I'd seen at the Hammonds'. But that didn't feel right—it would be saying something ugly about a neighbor, and Mama didn't want me to do that.

I liked visiting Mr. Mose. No matter when I stopped by, he was working hard but ready to talk. I'd visited him nearly every afternoon since he'd begun pasting together a cement-block foundation exactly level under a string.

"Are you going to do all the work yourself?" I'd asked a few days back, looking over the big piles of cement block and boards sitting around his yard.

"Might."

"How come you don't want any help?"

"Joe Leonard don't like strangers."

Every time Mr. Mose picked up a new block, he spit chewing tobacco at a piece of board in the middle of the square that his house was going to make.

"Is Joe Leonard your boy?"

Mr. Mose pointed. "Say howdy, Joe Leonard."

Joe Leonard was a beagle dog lying across the hood of Mr. Mose's pickup. He twitched one ear when he heard his name, but his eyes didn't open.

"How'd he get up there?" I said.

"My mistake." Mr. Mose put his trowel down and patted his pockets. He pulled out a cloth bag with a red drawstring, poked a finger in it, and scooped out some brown bits of tobacco. He hawked loud and turned his back to spit, and then he put in the new tobacco. "He's little, I put him up there to keep him out of the way, and he liked it. Learned how to do that hisself—derned if I know how with them short legs."

Joe Leonard's ears twitched again.

"Joe Leonard wants his own place right back there. I went ahead and marked it out so he'd quit aggervating me." He shook his head and spit again. I couldn't even tell where it hit, it was so dead center on top of the rest.

"My wife bought herself a Volkswagon to keep Joe off her car. He can't relax because the fenders is so round."

"Do you have any children?" I said.

"Nope."

"How come?"

"Got Joe Leonard."

"Dogs aren't family."

"Joe Leonard is."

"You didn't *have* him."

"I got him."

"You know what I mean."

"Yep." Mr. Mose wiped at his face. "I guess I know. You're asking what's none of your business. You ought to let it alone."

"I'm just figuring on it."

"On what?"

"Having babies. Everybody says something different, acts like it's nothing, acts like it's something."

"Well," Mr. Mose said.

"My Aunt Map says she wanted them and couldn't have them. Mama has me and Jo Lynn, and is having another one because nobody asked her. Mary Faith Hammond is having one and she's only fifteen."

"We-e-e-ll." He was looking off at the lake, then across the pasture at the Otwells', then back to the woods.

"Well *what*?"

"Well nothing." He slapped some cement on a

block and smoothed it out with a trowel. "That's my family there," he said, pointing at Joe Leonard.

"You've got a wife, don't you?" I asked.

"My wife don't live with me no more." Mr. Mose's voice was polite, like Mama's when she introduced me to a grownup. "We're getting a divorce."

Divorce was a word like *pregnant*—nobody ever said it right out. I was proud I didn't show any surprise. "Won't you be lonesome?" is what I said.

"I'm lonesome married," Mr. Mose said. "Won't be any more lonesome divorced."

He spit, but he was looking the other way and didn't hit the board.

Listening to Mr. Mose's hammering, I hunted around in the kitchen for something colored to spit. There wasn't any tobacco in our house, not even cigarettes left from Daddy. Finally I mixed up a handful of cocoa and sugar that looked about right. I wrapped it in waxed paper and went out to the sandpile to finish up a ranch I had started, with pine-cone trees and miles of twig fences, and a sand adobe house.

But as soon as I stepped out the kitchen door, I

saw Mary Faith Hammond way up the driveway walking toward Big Red at the fence. His head was tossing up and down like he was alarmed, but he let her touch him. He didn't back off. Nobody could touch Red except me and Daddy, but there he was with her hand on his nose and him not even fighting her off. Something was bad wrong, and there wasn't anybody home except me to see what it was.

Seven

I DIDN'T HAVE any choice but to go. I told myself that Mary Faith didn't know I'd seen what had happened at her house the other night, and the only thing to do was to act like I hadn't. Then I headed up the hill at a run. "What are you doing?" I yelled, but she didn't look around.

Then I saw the top strand of barbed wire cutting into the fleshy place at the base of Red's neck. He'd brought down two strands; they went around his front legs three or four times.

"He's caught—we've got to do something," Mary Faith said.

Red arched his neck and looked down his nose at her.

I looked at her too, and missed a step staring at the discolored places on her forehead and the bottom of her jaw that she'd tried to cake over with makeup. Her bruises shook me up so bad, I would have turned around and run straight back home if Red hadn't been standing there with his front legs caught in the barbed wire.

He was caught bad, and I had to do something about it. I took a deep breath and reminded myself again that Mary Faith didn't know I'd seen a thing. Then I concentrated on helping Red.

"We get him to pick his leg up, we can just slip this off, see, and then the other wires'll be loose enough to untangle," she said.

"That won't work. He can't get his leg high enough without being steadied, and we're not big enough to do that—he'd fall right over. Wait here." I took off to Mr. Mose's for help for the second time that week.

But before I was halfway across the pasture, I heard his truck driving off toward town.

"There's nobody here but us," Mary Faith called. "We got to do something before Red hurts hisself worse." She pressed her forehead against Red's nose, and he stood still as a statue, waiting for us to free him.

Mary Faith was right: There wasn't any help for Red but her and me. She was acting better about him than I was, and all of a sudden I was ashamed of wanting to find somebody else.

I walked back, thinking hard about how Daddy would run his hands along Red's neck and shoulder, then down his leg to the hoof. Red would lift a front hoof right back to him without a bit of trouble when he did that.

I tried—and Big Red tried. His hoof lifted as much as it could without the barbed wire cutting into him, then dropped back with a thud.

"You're bigger than me, so you have to be his leg, steady him what you can. Get right in here." I showed Mary Faith how to back into the hollow behind Red's front leg where his ribs started. "What he'll do is sway some of his weight against you when I pull that leg up."

Mary Faith was already braced, hunkering down with her back to him and her legs spread. "Okay," she said.

I talked to Red, patting him on the nose before I tried to pick up his hoof. He helped, lifting when he felt my hands pulling the wire. But when he lifted, the wire got tighter. He held for a while, but I couldn't get anything untangled. When he had to put his foot down, the wire stayed tight.

Mary Faith leaned against Red, her cheek resting on his shoulder.

"We're going to have to cut that wire," I said.

"Well, do it quick," she said. "He can't stand much more." Red swung his nose around to her.

I ran back to the old garage for the cutters. When I got back, Mary Faith was hanging around Red's neck with her face buried in his mane. "Easy, boy, easy," she said. "We'll have you out of here in no time."

The whites of Red's eyes were beginning to show, and he was breathing hard. I sawed at the wire with both hands on the cutters, making new silver nicks but not cutting through.

"Let me." Mary Faith grabbed the cutters. I held Red's nose and talked to him while she tried to cut through. After a while a wire sprang apart, unwrapping half a loop around Red's leg. He pulled back, his head going up and down, then stopped when the other loops tightened. "Easy, easy," I said, talking and humming while Mary Faith sawed some more, and another wire popped loose.

"Cut it one more time," I said, and she did. Her

and I and Red were all bleeding from cuts from the barbed wire. Then the wire slapped back against my blue jeans and Red was free. He backed up, his front feet tapping a dance on the ground and his head flapping from side to side like bird wings. Mary Faith walked toward him with her hand out, laughing.

"Watch out," I yelled, but she went right on, talking like he knew her. "There, boy, everything's okay now." Red's eyes rolled white, his ears went flat back, and he whirled away, bucked a few steps, and ran, Lady and Flash right behind him. Mary Faith was left standing there with her hand up to pet him. When she turned around, her face was away-looking, disappointed.

"He's just glad to be free," I said, to make her feel better. "Big Red's not much for petting."

She glanced back at the horses, then walked to the fence and kicked at the pieces of barbed wire lying in the grass. "I thought maybe he'd like me if I set him loose."

I laughed before I saw she meant it. "Horses don't think like that," I explained. "All he knows is he can run now. That's what he likes best."

With the excitement over I felt shy; I couldn't keep my eyes away from Mary Faith's face. There was a bruise on her upper arm, too, wide and striped, that went around it like a band. "How'd you get that?" I blurted out, pointing, before I could stop myself.

"I fell," she said, not looking at me. A hand went to her face, fingering the bad bruise along her forehead. "I fell down the steps at the kitchen door and hit my head."

"You *fell*—?" I snapped my mouth shut.

"I lost the baby, too, so I can ride now," she said. Her face stayed perfectly still and she didn't make a sound. But tears slid down her cheeks and ran toward the center of her chin until she reached up and wiped them away.

"I'm real sorry," I said. "Mama's having trouble keeping hers, too. She's having to stay in bed all the time. She wants that baby more than anything in the world. I'm sorry you lost yours."

"I landed on my stomach, see, when I fell, and the baby was hurt, and then it just came out of me." Both hands pressed against the middle of her lower stomach like it still hurt.

I felt sick, thinking of Mary Faith's own daddy hurting her and the baby that would have been his grandchild.

"Maybe now that you don't have to worry about the baby, you can ride Flash double with me sometime around the lakes," I muttered, because I didn't know what else to say.

MARY FAITH OFFERED to help nail some boards up where we'd cut the barbed wire. With both of us it wasn't so hard to do, and working with her felt good. We couldn't get the boards on straight, but we were pleased and stood admiring our work when Mama's car turned into the driveway. She stopped beside us and got out, looking at the fence and frowning. Jo Lynn stayed in the front seat staring straight ahead.

"What happened here?" Mama asked.

"Red got his leg caught in the fence. Me and Mary Faith had to cut him loose."

"Hello, Mary Faith." Mama nodded. To me she said, "Next time you wait. You could have been bad hurt. Where's Map?"

"Gone to get something she forgot."

Mama's lips were a thin line. "Well, I'm glad you put the boards up—at least we won't be chasing horses all over the countryside," she said, walking around to the car door slow, both hands on her stomach. "Thank you for helping, Mary Faith."

Mary Faith's eyes ran over Mama and Jo Lynn;

she threw back her head, her fingers flying up to touch her hair, and said in a bored voice, "I have to get home now. I'm expecting a phone call." I watched her walk over to the iron gate and force her way through.

THE WHOLE REST of the day went wrong. Jo Lynn griped that I'd been in her things and hadn't hung her twirler suit up right. Mama was mad at Map for leaving me alone, and at me for messing up the kitchen. I had to throw out the cocoa and sugar I hadn't spit, and I had to eat all my supper when I wasn't even hungry.

The first thing Map said when we sat down at the table was, "Mary Faith Hammond is not a fit companion for you. You're not to have anything to do with her."

"Why not?" I said, feeling mean enough to challenge her. "She was real good with Big Red."

"We have to take our help where we can get it, sometimes," Mama cut in, her voice tired and edgy. "But Map's right, Prin. Mary Faith is a little old for you, I think. You'd be better off with friends your own age. Why don't you ask Sarah Chaney to come home with you from church next Sunday?"

"I don't see why I can't be friends with Mary

Faith," I pressed. "Why's that wrong just because she's older?"

Map's mouth popped open, but Mama stopped her before she could say anything. "Mary Faith has different interests than you do, Prin," she began patiently. "She's got to think about her—baby—and you don't know about those kinds of things yet."

Map and Jo Lynn were both staring at her, surprised she'd said right out Mary Faith was going to have a baby. I tried to tell them different.

"I do know about things," I said. "And Mary Faith's lost—"

"I do not want to hear any more about Mary Faith Hammond. Now I think I've made myself clear on the subject," Mama cut in.

"I'm just trying to tell you she's—"

"Young lady, I have had enough out of you today! And I will not have you arguing with me," Mama exploded. "Do you hear me?"

"Yes, ma'am," I mumbled.

"Good. Then let's finish this meal in peace and quiet."

Eight

MR. B.Z. MENDED our fence right the next day. Mary
Faith must have told him about Red, or maybe he
saw the boards we'd nailed up crooked across the
hole in the barbed wire.

Around suppertime we heard Red whinnying
and stomping around, and Mr. B.Z. was prying
the boards off, then using his crowbar as a wedge
to twist together a splice in the barbed wire. Mama
and Map and me stood at the kitchen door watching, the two of them upset because he was taking

it on himself to be helpful, and me upset because I didn't ever want to see him again.

"I guess he'll expect to be paid now," Mama said when he finished and turned toward our house.

Seeing Mr. B.Z. coming toward the house scared me so bad, I wanted to hide in a closet. But if I did, I would miss everything, so when Mama and Map went out to talk to him I watched from the dining-room window, careful to stand far enough away not to stir the curtains.

Mr. B.Z. wouldn't take Mama's money. "It's like I said afore: I'll be glad to help out while Mr. Campbell's sick. That's what neighbors is for," he said.

"If you hadn't fixed it, I'd have had to ask one of the truck drivers to," Mama said in a cool business voice. "You should be paid the same as he would be." Her words and the money in her outstretched hand should have told Mr. B.Z. he was a hired hand and not a neighbor.

But the more Mama tried to put him off, the more he acted like he didn't notice, surprising us all by calling out, "Is that you, Miss Elizabeth?" right through the open window.

"Yes, sir," I said, wondering how he could have seen me. There wasn't anything to do but step up to the window and answer.

"I 'preciate you taking a interest in Mary Faith. She tells me y'all talk sometimes."

"Sometimes," I muttered.

"Well, she's right lonesome out here in the country. It's nice she's got somebody to talk to, 'specially somebody as nice as you."

"We don't talk much," I said in a hurry, wishing he hadn't brought that up in front of Mama and Map. "Just sometimes when I'm riding by and she's out in the yard." I didn't say in whose yard.

"Well, I 'preciate it." Mr. B.Z. nodded and tipped his cap at Mama. "Y'all jest call now, if there's anything else I can do," he said, and went home still without taking any money.

ABOUT A WEEK later I saw Mary Faith in Raleigh Springs. I had thought of her as having just me for a friend, and without a life other than right there on Coleman Road. So it was a shock to see her in Landis's Drugstore.

Map gave me a dime to get a soda at Landis's if I got through at the library before she and Jo Lynn were through at the grocery. I checked out my books quick and hurried over so I'd have plenty of time to look at the comics.

Landis's had big plate-glass windows and lots of dark wood and mirrors inside, and a polished white linoleum floor that was cool to sit on between the two turning wire racks of comics. It was usually full of high school boys who aggravated Mr. Landis because they never had any money to spend. When I came in that day, they were already at the soda fountain. Mary Faith must have come later, while I was reading a *Superman*; I didn't realize she was there until I heard her laugh.

She was standing with Sarah Chaney's big brother Dwight over by the cosmetics counter. But Mr. Landis's mirrors multiplied them on every wall in the store, so the boys at the fountain could see everything from where they sat. They watched, and I did, too, knowing by their sudden quiet that they had put Dwight up to talking to Mary Faith.

I couldn't hear what he said, but I could see what he did. He started off gentlemanly enough, holding Mary Faith's wrist and squirting a cologne sample on it to make her smile. But pretty soon he leaned over and said something that caused her to step back a pace and the boys at the soda fountain to nudge each other and snicker. Dwight held on to her wrist, spraying different colognes one on top of the other, and didn't let go when she pulled back the second time. Instead, he moved closer, pinning her against the counter and leaning his head down to whisper something that made her try to jerk past him. The boys snickered louder, one or two falling off their stools.

Whatever was going on, I didn't like it. Mary Faith had looked happy and pretty. Now her face was flaming red and she was about to cry. In the mirrors I could see some of the boys keeping Mr. Landis busy while Dwight pestered Mary Faith. There didn't seem to be anybody there to take her side except me.

But before I could stand up and call out her name, the front doorbell tinkled and Larry Hammond walked in heading for the soda fountain. Right away there was a change. The boys quit watching the mirrors and made room for Larry in the middle of their group, clapping him on the back and talking loud about basketball.

Dwight went back to the soda fountain quick, leaving Mary Faith rubbing her wrist and looking dazed. I scrambled to my feet to go see if I could help, but the doorbell tinkled a second time, and Jo Lynn walked in.

She hesitated in mid-step while the boys all turned to stare at her. Then she fixed a bright smile on her face and walked straight up to the counter, sending them scattering like she was a wind blowing in every direction. Even Larry Hammond slid off his stool so she could sit down. She gave him a big, brilliant smile that had nothing in it of the feelings I knew she had for Mary Faith, slid onto his stool, and ordered herself a cherry Coke.

The boys fell all over each other to say something to Jo Lynn that would make her laugh, but not one of them touched her or stood close enough to be fresh like Dwight had just been with Mary Faith. Jo Lynn laughed at everybody, including Larry Hammond. She was almost glowing, she was having such a good time.

But Mary Faith wasn't. She stood where Dwight Chaney had left her, rubbing her wrist and watching in the mirrors while her brother and Dwight Chaney and all those other boys laughed and cut up with Jo Lynn.

Then she put down the bottle of peroxide she'd meant to buy and tiptoed around the end of the counter toward the front door. When the bell tinkled, Larry looked around and saw her leaving. "Wait up," he called, but she slid on out.

Larry said something to the boys and Jo Lynn and ran out after his sister, Jo Lynn's eyes following him in the mirrors until he rounded the corner of the building.

I sat back down on the floor like the air had gone out of my legs. What I'd seen hadn't taken ten minutes, but I felt like I needed a year to think about it. But the doorbell tinkled again, and this time it was Map. Jo Lynn flounced out, giggling and waving over her shoulder at the boys, and I walked out behind her, my dime still in my hand.

THE NEXT AFTERNOON when I crawled into the cave, Mary Faith was already there, watching Larry and his friends play basketball. Without taking her eyes off the game, she pointed at the sack of candy at her feet, telling me to help myself.

While I was unwrapping a piece, I stole a look at her, wondering if I could get her to talk about being in the drugstore. She looked pretty and ordinary sitting there. Nothing about her helped me see why Dwight Chaney had treated her like he did.

"How's Red?" she asked, absentminded but friendly.

"He's okay. Has some bad cuts on his legs, but we put Vaseline on them and they're healing. What are you reading?" I asked, picking up the *True Confessions* magazine beside her. The cover had a picture of a woman with her head thrown back and her mouth open in a big O.

"That's none of your business," she said, and snatched it. "You're too young for that kind of stuff."

"I know more than you think," I said.

"I doubt that."

"I know what a good lay is." I still didn't know what that meant, but seeing Mary Faith with Dwight had reminded me he'd said that about her.

Mary Faith knew what it meant, though, and she took it personal. Her body went all stiff, and she didn't look at me. "Where'd you hear that, your snotty sister?"

"No."

"Where?"

"Nowhere."

"Jo Lynn told you. She's a liar."

"Didn't. Sarah Chaney told me. She's got all brothers, she hears lots of things." I didn't say Dwight's name right out, but I still held my breath, wondering if Mary Faith would put it all together.

While she thought, I leaned forward and squinted through the pines like I was interested in the basketball game. For a minute she sat hugging her arms around her knees and rocking down on her bare feet, then back on her seat that was just covered by short shorts.

"Is Dwight Chaney her brother?" she finally asked.

I nodded, waiting to see if she'd mention the drugstore.

"Well, he's a liar, too," she mumbled. "I didn't never do that with him."

"Do what? You didn't do what with Dwight?"

"It wadn't him," she said, louder. "I wouldn't go out with him if he asked me. I don't even *like* him. It ain't him."

"*What* isn't him?" I asked, but she still wouldn't say what she hadn't done with Dwight Chaney.

"I thought you knew some stuff." She stared at me, a cold, hard stare that was not friendly.

"I do," I muttered.

"Then I guess you know about French kissing."

"Sure."

"And dongs."

I shrugged.

"Red's got a big one. Biggest thing I've ever seen."

I didn't say anything.

"How about you?" she said.

"How about me what?"

"You seen anything bigger?" She was mad, and taking it out making fun of me.

"Sure."

"Who?"

"Who what?"

"Who's got one bigger?"

"Everybody I know," I said. "Everybody."

"Your old man? You seen your old man's pecker?"

"Sure," I said. "Hadn't you?"

Mary Faith's face twisted like cellophane; her breath came up unexpected. "You got an ugly mind," she muttered, wiping her eyes with the side of a finger. "And you're a liar, too. You don't know nothing about *nothing*. Dwight Chaney ain't my baby's daddy, and anybody's a liar that says he is."

I stared at her, not even trying to hide my surprise. Whoever had said Dwight Chaney was her baby's daddy? Then it hit me—that's what *a good lay* must mean, a girl who has had sex with a boy. That's why Mama had been so offended, and why Jo Lynn didn't want to be teased anymore about Dwight Chaney. She thought Dwight had had sex with Mary Faith.

But Mary Faith had just said she hadn't even been out with him, and said it so strong that I believed her. Suddenly the question of who *was* her baby's daddy hit me hard.

Mary Faith was watching the basketball players, her body curved in on itself in an angry hunch. For a long time we didn't speak to each other, me thinking over what she'd said and what it meant, and her muttering under her breath about liars.

After a while she talked louder, and about the basketball game. Finally she offered me another peppermint, like she was trying to apologize for getting so upset. My thinking eased up, and I began to be interested in the game too.

As usual, Larry Hammond was captain. He always took on somebody who was short or not too fast, and then somebody else who was good. There were at least two on each side, sometimes four or five. After they picked sides, one side took the ball out past a make-believe line and threw it in, and then it was all dust and elbows and the ball hitting dirt, slapping into hands, swishing through the net or twanging off the rim, and the boys whistling and yelling, like they were doing then.

"Watch it! Watch it, watch it—"

"Over here, Larry."

"Hey man, what are you doing?"

"Whooo-o-o-p! He's the man! The Man!"

"Pick it up and move it! Hell, my old lady's faster than you."

"God, it's hot."

"Well, take it out and shake it."

Then they all doubled over laughing and slapping at each other. I stole a look at Mary Faith. She was giggling too, and had a strange-sad little

smile on her face. "I wish I was a boy," she said,
like she hadn't been mad at me just a minute ago.

"Yeah, I'd like to play basketball."

"Girls can play ball. I play real good—Larry
taught me."

"Oh, yeah? Then what do you want to be a boy
for?"

She shrugged. "They get to do things. They can
earn money working, they have cars." She watched
for a minute. "They're big, strong. Can't nobody
do nothing to them."

I didn't say anything, knowing she was thinking of her daddy. We sucked on peppermints and
watched the boys play for a while. Then a car drove
up and three more boys piled out, one of them
Dwight Chaney.

Mary Faith made a hissing sound between her
teeth. "I think I'll go play some," she said, looking
at me like a dare.

She backed out of the cave on our side, where
none of the boys could see her, and went around
behind the court to the kitchen steps. She sat
there watching until Larry said, "You want to
play?"

"Sure."

"You're on my side," he yelled. "Bitsy, you

switch over." For a split second none of the boys moved; then they shifted and paired up to guard each other again. Except the boy guarding Mary Faith didn't play very close to her. Right away the game was different, quieter and less fun.

Mary Faith crouched low, dancing on her toes and leading with her eyes, almost, they looked so fierce and bright. She played outside and could dribble with either hand, passing to Larry when he was ready to just dump it in. She didn't miss a foul shot. When she fell down, she got up and dusted herself off and played harder.

Mary Faith played fifteen minutes or so real good. Then the other team made a basket and she took the ball out, looking right at me when she was walking to behind the line. "Watch this!" she yelled. Larry looked at the pines, then back to where she was throwing him the ball. He threw it back at her and raced under the net. But Mary Faith didn't throw it to him or anybody else, but dribbled low and fast, charging right at Dwight Chaney. She hit her shoulder into the middle of his stomach under his breastbone, and he was down, *splat*.

He didn't get up either, but lay there moaning and holding his stomach, trying to catch his breath.

"Serves you right, you liar," Mary Faith hissed.

She threw the ball to Larry and walked over to the kitchen steps, picked up her magazine, and went in without looking back.

Nine

JO LYNN HAD no secrets like Mary Faith had. Of course she wouldn't be married or pregnant at fifteen, but she wouldn't color her hair or fingernails, either, or play basketball and charge a boy and knock him down. Instead, she was learning the social graces from Map, who grabbed every opportunity to leave a mark on her and me. That's the way she put it.

"It's time you girls learned some of the social graces. Especially you"—she smiled at Jo Lynn, who smiled back. "Pretty soon you'll be going to ladies' parties, and dating, and then to college. You'll need to know how to act."

The graces covered everything, down to how to get in a car. Map wouldn't go in headfirst, like is natural. She went rear end first, then swung her legs in with her knees together. A lady *always* tucked her skirt in and sat with her knees together, even when they were covered up by a table. Map talked about knees with eyes of warning, and Jo Lynn tried to do right by them. Map said girls should never be alone in a public place, or spend time talking to grown men—they might get talked about; they should be friends only with girls who didn't get talked about. *Don't get talked about* was Map's favorite saying. "Look at poor Mary Faith Hammond," and her eyebrows lifted like we all shared a secret. Jo Lynn smiled back like she knew what the secret was, so I decided to see if she would tell me.

One afternoon while Mama was at the doctor's and Map was taking a nap, I followed Jo Lynn into her room, where she was listening to the radio and ironing.

"What's a dong?" I started off, knowing I'd have to give her a way to act superior before she'd even talk to me.

She folded up a sheet she had ironed and looked at me with her eyebrows up and her lips curled down. "Where'd you hear that?"

"Just around."

"You heard it up in the pines spying on the Hammonds. I've seen you come out." She snorted, sounding like Map.

"I'm just watching Larry Hammond play basketball," I said, surprised she'd seen me and hadn't told Map.

Jo Lynn hesitated a split second, then asked, "Larry's got a basketball court up there?" like she wasn't very interested.

"Other side of the pines," I said, nodding.

She missed another beat, then said, "Who plays?"

"Larry plays a lot. Some other boys come over on weekends." For a second I thought she was wanting to know if Dwight Chaney played; then I remembered Larry Hammond's name on her party list, and her eyes in Mr. Landis's mirror watching him run out the door after Mary Faith, and I had her.

"You like Larry Hammond, don't you?" I said, breaking out in a grin.

"Of course not," she snorted, but she blushed like I'd hit a sore spot.

"I saw you making eyes at him at the drugstore," I teased. "I bet you're just dying for him to come to your party."

"He's a Hammond," she said, slamming the iron down on its metal pad like she could stamp out his last name. "He may be good-looking *and* basketball captain, but he's still a Hammond. I couldn't ever go out with him."

Now we were down to what I wanted to talk about. So I said real nice, "Will you please tell me what's wrong with the Hammonds?"

"They're white trash." She shrugged. "Half the time they don't work, don't go to school like they ought to. B.Z. Hammond's done just about every sorry thing you can think of, and look at Mary Faith." She hung a skirt on a wire hanger, satisfied she'd made herself plain.

"Well, I'm looking. What about Mary Faith?" I asked, still trying to be patient. "What's wrong with her?"

"Well, there's girls and there's girls. Some have it, some don't."

"Have *what*?" I almost shouted, wishing she'd say right out what she meant.

"Class. They behave right."

"Well, what's behaving wrong?" I thought I knew, but wanted her to tell me in case I'd missed something.

She thought about it while she ironed a piece of lace around the collar of her best blouse. "Behaving wrong means doing everything Mary Faith does," she said, careful about every word. "Behaving right means not letting boys be fresh with you, not getting yourself talked about."

Like Dwight had been fresh with Mary Faith at the drugstore, I thought. And the boys at the soda fountain had been talking.

"But how can you help it? How can you stop somebody walking up to you and being fresh, or stop people talking? Anybody can talk about anybody they want to," I said. I'd seen it happen.

"Well, now you take your friend Mary Faith. She *asks* for it. Look at what she wears, look at her hair. She has pierced ears."

"So?"

"So—do you think Mama'd let us dye our hair?"

"Nope."

"Pierce our ears?"

"Mama wears earrings."

"Piercing's cheap."

"Why?"

"It just *is*. It's cheap, no class."

"Just looks like earrings to me."

"What do you know?" Jo Lynn folded her arms across her stomach exactly like Mama. "Look here, look at Mary Faith's shorts. Now you know not to wear short shorts."

"I don't have any. Besides, if I ride in short shorts, horse sweat gets in my crack."

"Short shorts show everything you've got," Jo Lynn said. "Short shorts get you *pregnant*, just like your friend Mary Faith Hammond. She's fifteen years old and she's not married and she's pregnant!"

"She is too married," I nearly shouted, saying what I knew wasn't true, I was so mad at Jo Lynn's acting like Mary Faith was worse than dirt.

Jo Lynn stared at me like I was an idiot. "Who told you that?"

"She did," I mumbled, sorry I'd brought it up.

"Ha! She's no more married than I am. If she is, where's her ring? Where's her husband?"

I glared back at her, cornered. "She doesn't have to be married anymore, because she's not going to have a baby. She fell down some steps and hurt it and it came out of her dead."

Jo Lynn looked like the air had been taken out of her, and turned her back to search for something in the clothes basket.

I didn't want to go on either, but there was one more question I had to ask. "Well if she's not married, who's the daddy of her baby?"

"Don't ask me, ask her," Jo Lynn mumbled. "With a girl like that it could be anybody."

I turned my back on Jo Lynn, disgusted. Now I understood why she and Map disliked Mary Faith so. It was as much for a thing she couldn't help— her last name—as for being pregnant and not married. They didn't care that Mary Faith couldn't help who her father was or what he did. Or that she didn't have a mother and aunt to teach her not to get pregnant or wear short shorts and too much makeup. They cared that she looked "cheap." And they acted like looking cheap was catching, something I might get just by being her friend.

LATER THAT DAY I walked over to see Mr. Mose and scratch Joe Leonard's ears. But for once Mr. Mose didn't want to talk, except about the trucks.

"I see one of your daddy's dump trucks parked there behind the house," he said. "If it ain't busy, you tell your mama to send me two loads of gravel so this driveway won't go to mud next time it rains."

I said I would, then climbed back over the fence and trotted toward the Hammonds'. My feelings about Mary Faith were so mixed up, I crawled into the pine cave without looking, then nearly yelled. She was there waiting, and she was excited.

"I was hoping you'd come over," she said, grabbing my arm. "I got something to show you."

"What is it?"

"It's in the house. Come on, nobody's home."

I would have said no in a second if Mr. B.Z. had been there. But Mary Faith said he wasn't, and I was curious to see what she was so excited about.

I didn't go through the gate where Map or Jo Lynn could see me, but crawled under the fence and ran across Larry's basketball court to the kitchen door Mary Faith was holding open.

I'd never been in a house like the Hammonds'. The kitchen was dirty—not just dishes, but socks on the floor and ghost dust rolling around under a table with a splotched red-plastic top and metal rim that had dirt in the ridges. I could almost feel something breathing on my ankles. In the dining room paper was sagging off the ceiling around the light socket, and there were no curtains on the windows, only shades.

Mary Faith cut down the hall to her room, which was nicer than the rest of the house. Everything was in its place, and pink plastic curtains hung at the windows. My ankles quit feeling like something was sliding around them. There was a stack of *True Confessions* in the corner, and a big, big old brown teddy bear with one eye gone on Mary Faith's bed. She shut the door.

"Look here." She took a cut-flat grocery sack off a card table in the corner, and the picture of Red was underneath, taped to the table. She'd painted him in a trot, with opposite feet coming forward, his tail and mane wisping back and his head high. It was exactly Red, like a photograph.

"You did that? All from memory?"

"Well, I see him every day," she said, shy and proud. "I studied him, and I practiced. This is the fifth picture I done."

"Wow, that's good! How'd you learn to do that?"

"Mostly in school." She shrugged. "Miss Gates showed me about watercolors. They're cheap and don't smell, like oil paints. Look here." She showed me pictures of flowers and Otwell's Lakes and the old shed behind her house.

"You ought to sell these," I said. "You could make lots of money."

"Who to?" she said, smiling a little. "I don't know nobody."

"Maybe you can set up a booth on the road and have an art show."

"Nobody comes by here. I could set out there a month and sell nothing."

"Maybe at our church bazaar, then. Everybody

brings things they make, and everybody else buys them."

"When's that?"

I tried to think when. "I don't remember. But we can find out. Why don't you come to church with us one Sunday, and we'll ask around."

"I couldn't do that."

"Sure you can. Anybody can go to church."

Mary Faith looked at the pictures like they were all new to her, then stacked them carefully on the foot of the bed with sheets of clean typing paper in between.

"Well, they're sure good. Especially Red," I said.

Mary Faith traced a wisp of Red's mane with her finger. "What time is church?" she said.

"We leave about eight-thirty. You just flag us down anytime you want to go. I—"

But Mary Faith wasn't listening to me. Her head was cocked toward her window, and the sound of a car door slamming. In no time there were steps on the front porch.

"Come on." She grabbed my arm and started hauling me toward the door.

"Who—"

"Come on!"

Before we got around her bed, her door slammed open, rebounded off the wall, and slammed back

again, then a third time before Mr. B.Z. Hammond was all the way in the room. His upper lip
was drawn up off his teeth, his hands busy with
his belt and the button to his pants. He was half
unzipped before he looked around and saw me
standing there with Mary Faith. She took two short
steps and stopped between me and him.

He looked from her to me and back again, cleared
his throat, and said, "Excuse me, Miss Elizabeth,
I didn't know Mary Faith had company." He quit
fooling with his pants, but he didn't zip them back
up. I turned back to stare at Red's picture so he
could do that without me watching.

"How y'all getting along?" he said.

"Just fine."

"Jest fine?" he mimicked. "Jest fine without a
man around to do for you? Your mama don't think
all you women need a man around?" Mr. B.Z.'s
voice asked a meaner question than his words, but
I didn't have to answer—Mary Faith broke in.

"Prin was just leaving," she said. "She's got to
go home now."

I turned around in time to see Mr. Hammond
giving Mary Faith a look that shrank her back a
step or two. But when he went on, he was talking
more polite. "I'm glad you come to visit. How about
some iced tea?"

"No, thank you."

"Mary Faith, you fix us some tea."

"She said she don't want any. She's got to get home," Mary Faith said.

Mr. Hammond still hadn't fastened up his pants. He looked from me to Mary Faith and back again, grinning like he enjoyed catching us in a room we couldn't get out of unless he let us. I looked down at Big Red's picture, but he wasn't dancing anymore. He looked like I felt—trapped.

"That's all there is to see," Mary Faith said, snatching up a grocery sack and slapping it over the picture. "You better go on home now—I'm tired of playing with you," she said straight in my face. "You're too little." Her eyes were not mean, but scared, begging me to leave.

"Mary Faith, you better watch your manners," Mr. B.Z. was saying, his voice as quiet as Mama's snake voice. "I told you to get us some tea."

"She don't want any."

"You better do what I say."

She looked at him, her face hateful but her body stiff and scared.

I was scared, too, at the bad feelings they aimed at each other, and at the way Mr. B.Z. looked at me. "I better get on home now," I said, barely whispering. "Mama'll be wanting me." I took a step toward the door, but Mr. B.Z. slumped against the doorframe and he didn't move. His right hand squeezed the front of his trousers, his fingers inside the flap.

I couldn't think of a thing to say to get him to step aside.

Then he straightened up. He nodded at me, grinning, and said, "You excuse my daughter's manners, you hear? You're welcome back anytime—we'd be proud to have you."

"Yes, sir."

I edged toward the door, Mary Faith right beside me. Mr. B.Z. turned sideways, not taking his hand off the knob and not clearing the way enough so we could get by without brushing against him.

Mary Faith was crying. "You old bastard," she muttered, her teeth gritted together.

"What?" Mr. Hammond called down the hall. "What'd you say to me?"

Mary Faith pushed me ahead of her, almost running through the kitchen and down the steps, the door slamming to behind us, cutting off him yelling, "Mary Fa—"

She kept her hand on my shoulder, marching me to the gate. "Not this way—Map'll see me," I said. But she didn't pay attention, and I couldn't

break her hold on my arm before she got to the
gate and pushed me through.

MAP SHOT OUT the kitchen door and grabbed me at
the edge of the patio. "Did I see you running out
of Mary Faith Hammond's backyard?" she yelled.

I didn't have time to think, I was so surprised
at trouble being in front of me instead of behind.

"I've told you a thousand times not to go in those
people's house," Map yelled.

"You never did," I said, still trying to catch my
breath from running home. "You—"

"Don't you sass me, young lady. Don't you lie
to me either." She shook me.

"You told Jo Lynn," I said. "You never told me
nothing. And—"

"Anything," she yelled.

"And Mary Faith's just showing me some pictures of Red she'd painted."

"I meant the both of you and you know it. You
know you're not supposed to have anything to do
with that girl."

"Mary Faith's lonesome." I would have told even
Map about Mary Faith's house if she would have
listened. But she kept on yelling.

"That's her problem."

"I'll go where I want to," I yelled, not able to stop myself. "You can't tell me what to do—you're not my mama."

"As good as," she shouted. "You'll show me some respect, young lady, or you'll wind up in your room for the rest of the summer with your seat too hot to sit on."

"You're a fearsome old woman," I shouted back. "You don't talk real, you—"

Map slapped me. Her hand flashed out and swatted my face, snapping my head back so I stumbled against the house, my head cracking against the asbestos shingles.

When I could see Map again, she was holding her face with both hands and stumbling toward the kitchen door. "Oh, my Lord," she was saying to herself. "What have I done?"

Ten

I COULDN'T SLEEP that night, but lay wrapped in my sheet watching the stars and listening to the horses. They stopped in the valley just below my window like they were waiting for me, and after a while I slipped out.

Flash let me swing up and lie draped along her neck and back while she grazed, almost like she knew how bad I felt. She smelled horsey and felt warm and good, following Red around the front pasture close enough for me to lean out and touch him.

But that night even riding couldn't calm me down; Mr. B.Z.'s undone zipper and Map's slap crashed around in my head without leaving space to sort things out. I'd been spanked, but never hit in the face before. Map hadn't bruised me like Mr. B.Z. had Mary Faith, and I was more mad than hurt. But I understood a little better why Mary Faith was afraid of her daddy. I decided I had to talk to Mama about what happened this time, even if she didn't want to listen.

But I overslept the next morning, which was Sunday. Before I even finished dressing, Jo Lynn cornered Mama to complain that my socks didn't match and my dress wasn't starched crisp enough for church. After breakfast I changed socks for the third time and sneaked outside to where I wouldn't hear her carrying on or have to talk to Map. I'd have to wait till after church to get Mama alone and tell her what was going on.

I was careful not to get sand on my shoes while I checked on the village I was building out of wet sand. Then something moved up front and caught my eye, and there was Mary Faith coming out her back gate in a glittery pink dress. When she got to the shade of our pine trees, she stood there. Just seeing her made the skin on my arms prickle. When she waved, I barely waved back.

It wasn't until we were in Map's car that I remembered telling Mary Faith she could go to church with us. "Wait, stop!" I said, speaking to Map for the first time that morning.

She stopped the car so quick I slid off the backseat.

"What is it?" she asked, stretching to see over the hood. "Is something in the road?"

"No, ma'am, it's just—Mary Faith's going to church with us." I held my breath, waiting for her to explode.

"She's what?"

"She's going to church with us. She's up there waiting." I pointed.

Map and Jo Lynn stared straight ahead. "My word," Map said. Jo Lynn made a sound in her throat.

"Everybody needs to go to church, Mama says, so I asked her," I said in a rush.

"Well, I never." Map just sat there.

"I didn't think she'd come," I muttered.

"Jo Lynn, you'll have to take her to your class," Map said, surprising her and me both.

"I can't go to church with Mary Faith," Jo Lynn whispered. "I'll never hear the last of it."

"Oh, hush up," Map said, letting the car roll forward a little. "She's too old to go to the juniors class with Prin. She belongs in intermediates with you. Taking somebody to church never hurt anybody's reputation."

"I won't."

"You will," Map said, picking up speed. "You'll act like a lady and make her welcome, treat her like she was a guest in your own home."

I was surprised at Map not blowing up at me and then standing up to Jo Lynn, but that wasn't enough to stop my being mad at her.

She pressed on the gas and leaned over the steering wheel to stare at Mary Faith, who smoothed her hair two or three times. "Look at that dress," she whispered. It had a square neck and puffed sleeves and a long full skirt, and glittered every time Mary Faith breathed.

When we got up beside Mary Faith, Map pasted a smile on and shot a look at Jo Lynn, who was sitting in front of me, so I couldn't see her face. I opened the back door and scooted across the seat saying, "Hi. Crawl in back here with me." I sounded fakey even to myself.

Mary Faith got in headfirst on Jo Lynn's side of the car.

"Good morning, Mary Faith," Map said in her schoolteacher voice. "We're glad to have you join us this fine Sunday morning."

"Good morning, Mrs. Map."

"Porter. My name is Mrs. Porter."

Mary Faith blushed.

"Good morning, Mary Faith," Jo Lynn said, turning all the way around to smile at Mary Faith. "My Sunday school class will be glad you're visiting this morning."

Mary Faith looked at me, her eyes wide and scared.

"Aunt Map thinks you ought to go with the intermediates," I explained, turning my hands up to show I couldn't help it.

"You already know some of the girls, Mary Faith," Jo Lynn said. She kept up a chatter about school, with Map putting in a sentence or two when she ran down.

I sat in my corner of the backseat, glad they were doing the talking. Mary Faith sitting right there beside me brought yesterday back too strong. It was hard to look her in the face.

Mary Faith was pretty with her hair pulled back and not too much makeup on, but something wasn't quite right about her dress—not for church. She sat with her knees together, but she wasn't wearing hose, and her shins were nicked and scraped. Her hands were empty, too; she hadn't brought a Bible or purse or gloves, and when she unclenched her fist to smooth her hair, I saw dirt under her fingernails.

From the first minute we walked in, church was miserable. My and Jo Lynn's friends didn't know what to say to Mary Faith, so they didn't talk or sit with us. The grownups were worse, acting like they were happy she'd come, and treating Jo Lynn like she was a saint for bringing her. I wouldn't have asked her to go if I'd known she was going to be treated that way. In the car going home we couldn't look at each other, we felt so bad. I hadn't remembered to find out about her selling pictures at the bazaar, and I bet she hadn't either.

Map and Jo Lynn couldn't wait to tell Mama. "You'll never guess who went to church with us," Map said before the screen door banged shut behind her. "You'll never guess who Prin invited to church."

"Who?" Mama said, putting the last glass of iced tea on the table.

"Mary Faith Hammond. She was waiting for us at the top of the drive in a party dress."

"Is that right, Princess? When did you ask Mary Faith to go to church?"

Map and Jo Lynn both stopped and turned I-told-you-so faces toward me. All of a sudden I was in a hard place, and I wasn't ready. "Yesterday,"

I said, my eyes going to Map. She faded back a step, looking out the window like she could see yesterday coming down the drive. "We were talking about the church bazaar and I asked her to come to Sunday school."

I rushed ahead, thinking of a way to stick up for Mary Faith and me both. "You said asking people to church is always all right, so why's everybody so upset?"

But Mama wasn't going to let me off the spot. "Do you talk to her very much? You don't ever go into her house, do you?" She sat down at her place, watching me close.

"No, ma'am." My stomach moved around like I'd swallowed that lie and any second I'd throw it right back up. Map's mouth opened, then closed. A queer look ran across her face, and she walked quick to the refrigerator and looked in it for something.

"Good," Mama said, then added, "And stay away from B.Z. Hammond altogether."

"Yes, ma'am."

Map slammed the refrigerator door. She couldn't say I was lying without me telling Mama she had slapped me, and I knew she didn't want Mama to know that. So I just stared at her, feeling mean and glad she was caught in a lie too.

"Well, how did it go?" Mama was saying. "Jo Lynn, did she go to Sunday school with you?"

"Yes, ma'am."

"Well?"

"I tried to make her feel at home. I introduced her to everybody, showed her what to do in church. I declare, I don't think she'd ever been before."

"Jo Lynn carried on a conversation just like they were best of friends," Map said, clearing her throat. "She acted like a little lady."

"She lied," I said, angry at how they were talking about Mary Faith.

Everybody looked at me.

"Mary Faith's not your friend—you aren't even going to invite her to your party. Behind her back you act like she's dirt."

"Prin." Mama sounded tired.

"She acted just right," Map said. "When a lady's put in an unpleasant situation with questionable people, she goes right on being a lady."

"That's acting a lie," I said.

"Well, would you have invited her if you'd expected anything else?" Map said, red spots growing on her cheeks. "Would you have wanted us to act any other way?"

She had me there; I couldn't think of a thing to say that was the truth.

"Map's right, Princess," Mama cut in. "People live together by having ways—having the social graces—to deal with unpleasant situations. Why, if we all told the whole truth to each other, we'd have a hard time living together, and we're family."

I glared at Map, red in the face and almost crying because she was acting a lie, pretending she hadn't lost her own social graces and slapped me. Jo Lynn had acted a lie about Mary Faith too, and everybody said that was all right. But my *telling* one wasn't.

Even though I'd wanted to tell Mama what had happened in Mary Faith's room, now that I'd lied to her I knew I couldn't. I picked at my dinner and wished again I could get to Daddy. Something dark was moving up close to my back, and he was the only one left who'd know how to stop it.

IF DADDY HAD been home, he could have stopped Mr. B.Z. from bothering Mama about the trucks, too. Lately Mama was talking all the time on the telephone to people Daddy did business with. But she was not able to get more work. Luther turned his truck in first, then two more came in the next week, and finally Daddy's foreman, Odell, got through with the last job, delivering gravel for Mr.

Mose's driveway, and lined his truck up with the other three in the parking space behind Daddy's office. Mama gave Odell a paycheck and let him go, thanking him for trying to help her make the business work without Daddy.

The next morning while I was dusting the living room, Mr. B.Z. walked up to our front porch.

I stared through the screen door at him.

"Morning, Miss Elizabeth," he said, grinning at me like we were buddies. "I sure did enjoy talking with you the other day. I think you and me's going to be friends, don't you?"

I couldn't answer.

"Is somebody here, Prin?" Mama called from the back hall.

I ran to get her, glad not to have to talk to Mr. B.Z. myself.

"I come to help," he told Mama right off.

"Help with what?" she asked, this time not even pretending to be friendly.

"With the trucking," he answered, leaning so close, the bill of his cap scraped the doorframe. "Everybody knows you got troubles, Miss Ada. And that's what neighbors is for, to help out when trouble comes. Your Elizabeth and my Mary Faith is friends, they visit together all the time, and I don't see why you and me cain't be. I could be real helpful to you."

"You've overstepped yourself, Mr. Hammond," Mama snapped, her voice cold as ice. "Any troubles I have are a private concern. I don't want your help."

Mr. B.Z. couldn't pretend any longer that Mama wasn't being downright rude. He stepped back from the screen door, jerking up his pants.

"That's mighty tall talk from a woman living alone," he growled, not friendly himself anymore. "Seems to me all kinds of things could go wrong when a woman don't have a man around to help out."

"Things like what, Mr. Hammond? Make your meaning clear," Mama shot back.

"Just *things*, Miss Ada." He shrugged, his upper lip curling in a sneer. "But you think you can take care of your own troubles, so I won't bother with you no more. I can see where I'm not wanted."

"Good. I'm glad you finally see that clear," Mama said. "Now if you'll excuse me, I have work to do." And she banged our front door shut before he had time to turn away.

Mama waited until she heard him walking off before she turned to me, her face like a thundercloud. "What does he mean, you and Mary Faith visit all the time?" she asked.

"I was in Mary Faith's room a couple of days ago—before you told me not to go to her house," I rushed, glad to finally let it all out. "Mr. B.Z. was there, and he scared me."

"What? When? What were you doing in the Hammonds' house?" she asked, alarmed.

I told her everything, including Map slapping me. I even went back and told her Mary Faith had lost her baby because her daddy shoved her down the kitchen steps. The only thing I didn't tell her was that I *saw* him shove her; I didn't see any reason to make things harder on myself by admitting I'd been night riding.

Mama sat on the sofa without moving, her face changing color. She looked sick.

But I already felt better. No matter how bad Mama worried or how mad she was for what I'd done, I was glad she finally knew everything.

"You know you'll have to be punished," Mama said after a while. "You told me a lie. You went where you must have known I didn't want you to go. And you've kept secrets, things you should have let me know about long ago."

"I tried to tell you," I muttered. "But you wouldn't listen."

Mama's eyes squeezed shut like she was reading something on her eyelids. When they snapped open, she'd made up her mind.

"I guess you're right, I didn't listen. I'm sorry, Princess. The next time you try to tell me something, I will.

"But you still have to be punished for the lie. You're not to ride for two whole weeks. You'll not play with the horses, or brush them, or do anything but be sure they have water. You can't go to the library, or talk or visit with any of your friends. That's your punishment.

"This part's not punishment, but you're not to have anything to do with Mary Faith or any of the Hammonds ever again. Is that clear?"

"Yes, ma'am."

"Do you understand why?"

I hesitated.

"There's all kinds of people in this world, Prin. Most are like your daddy and me, trying to be the good side of ourselves. There are some people who can't do that, some who don't want to. B.Z. Hammond is one of them. He's done great harm to his daughter because he hasn't loved her the way a father should. And I don't want you close to something that bad. It might spill over on you."

She took a deep breath, hands pressed against her stomach like the baby was kicking her. "B.Z. won't be back here bothering us after what I just said to him, either. You can forget about him.

"And Map owes you an apology. I'll see that she makes it," she added, her face set hard. "In *this* house we don't hit children in the face."

"You spank us," I said, wondering how I could last for two whole weeks without riding.

"You deserve it sometimes," she said. "But we've never left a bruise on you. And when you're spanked it's always on your seat and for something you've done that you shouldn't, never because Daddy and I are angry about something in our own lives, or just feel mean and want to hurt you some way, like B.Z. wants to hurt Mary Faith. There's a big difference."

I let her think I agreed, and I guess I did.

I felt better after talking to Mama, but she seemed to feel worse. What I'd told her had made her uneasy about Mr. B.Z.; she was worried about making him mad by telling him to leave us alone, too. That was why she started locking all our doors even in the daytime.

THE TWO WEEKS dragged by. I didn't ride, I didn't tease Jo Lynn about anything, and I didn't sneak to the pine cave to talk to Mary Faith. I missed her a lot, and was worried about how Mr. B.Z. was treating her.

Toward the end of the second week Map took me to a concert at Overton Park, where she bought me two bags of popcorn and apologized for slapping me. The popcorn was the best thing about the concert; that and hearing the Lone Ranger song in real music. It was called "The William Tell Overture."

But I wasn't fooled about getting to go to the concert. Mama didn't let me go just to make up with Map; she let me go because things were so dull we were all bored, and because Jo Lynn was doing something she wasn't supposed to do either, which was go on a real date before she was sixteen.

As soon as Goose Jamison asked her to the Methodist wienie roast, Jo Lynn forgot all about having a party for her good and special thing.

"You're going to let her go on a date!" Map said when Mama told us.

"It's with the Methodists," Mama answered. "Besides, it won't cost money like a party would."

"I bet they play spin-the-bottle in the Fellowship Hall. I bet that's why Jo Lynn has been practicing kissing," I said.

Mama looked surprised. "She's what? Practicing how?"

"On the hall mirror," I said. "She practices standing real close and kissing herself in the mirror. That's funny, isn't it?"

"Well—" Mama cut her eyes at Map and tried not to laugh. "I guess lots of girls do that. Don't tease your sister, Prin. You keep quiet about seeing her."

"Why do people kiss?" I said, grateful she was feeling good; it had been a long time since we'd laughed about anything together.

"Because they like each other a lot. You don't kiss everybody, just somebody you like special. You'll probably be about sixteen then. Or older, if I'm lucky." Mama laughed.

"Why don't you take a ride before supper?" she added. "We've got a treat tonight—Map bought a watermelon for dessert."

SINCE IT WAS my first day to ride again, I went around Otwell's Lakes twice, jumping a few rabbits and a covey of bobwhites before I felt satisfied and let Flash turn toward home.

While she held a fast, smooth pace up Coleman Road, I lay on her neck pretending I had to duck branches so I wouldn't be pushed off over a cliff.

Leaning down that way I didn't see Mr. B.Z. until
Flash snorted and slowed down. He was walking
toward us from his mailbox.

I pulled Flash up sharp, my skin crawling, my
heart pounding so loud I could hear it. I looked
up and down the empty road in a panic, for the
first time in my life wishing we had more neighbors.

"That sure was a long ride you took. I's about
to think you'd got throwed off," Mr. B.Z. said,
stopping in the middle of the road.

I didn't know how to get away from Mr. B.Z.
Flash was fighting the bit trying to go on home; I
didn't think I could get her to turn around and go
back to the lakes. Mr. B.Z. stood in front of our
pasture gate smiling and watching us turn in circles.

"You ain't been riding the last coupla weeks,
have you?" he said.

"No, sir," I answered, scared that he'd noticed.

Flash backed up a few steps, then started forward again. I wrapped a rein around each hand
and pulled back, barely able to stop her.

"Your pony's kinda feisty, ain't she? You sure
you can handle her?" He walked toward us with
his hand out.

"Yes, sir, I can handle her. She's just ready to

get on home," I said, but he didn't step aside. I backed Flash up some more, my arms getting tired from her pulling against the bit.

"I thought I seen you out one night riding in the dark, on your place."

"No, sir," I lied.

"No?" He watched me, his eyebrows up. I shook my head. "Well, I coulda swore it was you," he said. "Who do you reckon it was?"

"Nobody. The horses wouldn't let anybody but me get around them at night, but it wasn't me. Probably you just thought you saw something— moondark'll do that to you."

He laughed. "Well, maybe so."

I couldn't look him in the eye without showing how scared I was, so I leaned over like I had to untangle the reins.

"Don't fall off!" he yelled, and jumped toward me so quick Flash reared up and almost threw me off backward. When I got myself straightened up, Mr. B.Z. grinned at me from not two feet away, one hand on Flash's bridle and the other tucking the mail up under his arm.

"You're a real good rider," he said, patting Flash's neck and coming closer. "Most girls would have been throwed off."

I didn't say anything, busy acting like I was settling myself, but really kicking Flash on her far side so she pulled Mr. Hammond around in circles.

"I jest stopped to ask how y'all are gettin' on," he said, holding on to Flash's bridle while we all went round and round. "You being a friend of Mary Faith's and all, I thought maybe you'd set your mama straight about me. She shouldn't oughta treat me like she done—whoa, there, hoss—it ain't neighborly. I's jest trying to be helpful."

"Yes, sir," I whispered, my voice catching. My heels were beating Flash's flank so hard, the whites of her eyes were beginning to show.

"I said whoa, hoss," Mr. Hammond growled at Flash, yanking on the bit. She pulled back, making the mail drop from under his arm. "Whoa, dammit!" he yelled, smashing a fist down on her nose. She jumped, then stood there tense and trembling, a dribble of blood running down the side of her mouth. I was holding on to the saddle horn with both hands and trembling too, my mouth so dry, I couldn't have yelled if I'd wanted to. There wasn't anything I could do to get away from Mr. B.Z. Hammond inching closer and closer.

He dropped a hand over mine on the saddle horn and kept on talking, his other hand still holding Flash's bit in a tight grip that twisted her neck sideways. "Like I say, she ain't got no call to be mean to me. Living out here jest makes women-folks lonesome, now don't it? Hell, we all git lone-some, ever'body needs friends. I was real proud you come to visit Mary Faith, and I's jest trying to return the compliment being nice to your mama. I don't know why she's took up so against me."

I was almost in tears, trying to slide off the saddle away from him, except he still held my hands. "I— I don't know either. I'll tell her what you said just as soon as I get home. You can let go now."

"Let's jest let the pony settle down a little bit."

"She's settled, she's all right," I said, the tears spilling down my face. "I need to go home."

But Mr. B.Z. was listening to something else with his head a little to the side. I listened too, and we both looked up the road till Mr. Mose's pickup truck topped the hill. Mr. B.Z. let go of the bridle and stepped back quick, bending to get his mail scattered across the road. Flash wheeled and trotted to the gate before Mr. Mose slowed to a stop beside us.

"Is anything wrong?" he asked, sticking his head out the window.

I was shaking too hard to say a word.

Mr. Hammond nodded and said, "Miss Elizabeth was having a little trouble with her pony, there. Just about got herself throwed off."

"Well, I guess it was lucky you were here to help," Mr. Mose said, the tone of his voice saying just the opposite. "Are you all right, Miss Prin?" he added.

I nodded, hoping he wouldn't drive off until I was through the gate.

But he stayed right there and said in a cool voice, "B.Z., open that gate so she won't have to get off her pony."

"I'll be glad to," Mr. B.Z. said, and jumped to it.

Mr. Mose watched him through slitted eyes, his truck's big engine purring. "I was just on my way to see your mama, Miss Prin. I have a hauling job for her. You tell her I'll be over soon's I drop off this cement."

"Yes, sir."

Mr. B.Z. took the loop off the pasture gate and let it swing open. "You 'member what I said," he whispered when Flash trotted by. "Women living alone needs friends."

I kicked Flash hard, my heart in my throat, and in two steps we were galloping toward home.

I WENT STRAIGHT to the bathroom. I needed a bath. I was still shaking, and I felt dirty outside and in.

B.Z. Hammond had touched me.

He had just cost my last good thing about the summer, too: now I was too scared to ride out our front gate to get to Otwell's Lakes, because he might be waiting.

Mr. Mose was talking to Mama in the living room when I got through with my bath. As soon as he left, she came into my room and sat down on the bottom bunk. "Mr. Mose tells me you and Mr. Hammond had a little talk today, Princess. What about?"

I was glad she asked. "About your not being nice to him about the trucks. He said he was just trying to be neighborly, and you don't have any call to treat him mean. He said women alone need friends."

"Did he say anything else? Anything—fresh?" Mama's face looked grim. "Did he say or do anything he shouldn't have, Princess?"

"Yes, ma'am, he did. He wouldn't get out of the road and let me pass. He put his hand over mine on the saddle horn." I was trembling again just remembering.

For a minute Mama couldn't say anything. Then she came over and put her arms around me, rubbing between my damp shoulder blades with the soft palm of her hand.

"That won't happen again, Princess. Mr. Mose

has offered to put in a gate to the road on his side of the pasture. That way you can still ride around the lakes and won't run into Mr. Hammond at the mailbox. Is that all right?''

"Yes, ma'am." I hugged her, grateful that she had found a way for me to keep riding around Otwell's Lakes and still be safe from Mr. B.Z.

I went to bed feeling some better. But I woke up from a bad dream slick with sweat, my toes hooked into a wrinkle in the sheet. And I had to go to the bathroom from eating too much watermelon.

Mama and Map were still sitting in the living room, so it couldn't have been too late. I stuck my head around the corner to let them know I was up, then drew back when I heard what they were talking about.

"Well, are you going to call the sheriff?" Map was asking in a sharp whisper.

"And tell him what? That B.Z. stopped Prin on a public road and talked to her? Where's the crime in that?''

"He *threatened* us, Ada Ruth! He threatened that child—she's just too innocent to know it!"

"I know that!" Mama snapped. "But what can I do about it?''

After a time Map said, so low I almost couldn't hear, "I guess it's all true, then, everything I've ever heard about B.Z. Hammond being a sorry, no-account wife beater."

Mama took a deep breath. "I wouldn't be surprised if more than that's true, Margaret Ann. I wouldn't be surprised if B.Z. Hammond was the father of his own grandchild."

Somewhere inside, I guess I had figured that out the day Mr. B.Z. barged into Mary Faith's room unzipping his pants. But hearing Mama say it almost knocked me over. I slumped against the wall, so stunned and sorry for Mary Faith that the hall dark seemed to be coming from inside my own head.

When I heard Mama locking the front door behind Map, I hurried toward the bathroom because I didn't want to see her. But when I came out, she was a silhouette leaning against the open back door looking out at the moon. I could see the side of her face and her stomach holding her gown out from her body. "Too much watermelon, Princess?" she said. "The baby's restless tonight. Come feel it."

I walked over and put my arms around her. My ear rested on her stomach, and I felt the baby turning and poking like it was searching for a door. I heard it, too, a watery, humming sound somewhere between a stomach rumble and a heartbeat.

The baby was safe inside Mama, eating her food and using her warmth, just like I had before I was born. Mama would stay in bed or do anything she had to to keep it safe. But after it was born and grew up, it wouldn't be safe at all.

"Elizabeth?" Mama said, as soft as a dream, and ran her hand down the side of my face. "Are you crying?"

"It's just yawn tears." I stepped around the patch of moon on the floor and passed her.

Eleven

JO LYNN ALMOST missed the Methodist wienie roast. She spent the whole last week in July getting ready, polishing her fingernails and ironing her blouse and pedal pushers until they were shiny with starch. I hung around teasing her about kissing Goose good night, glad something was going on that would take my mind off Mary Faith and Mr. B.Z.

The day before the wienie roast me and Mama had to take Jo Lynn to the beauty parlor. She'd rolled her hair up in her hairbrush to see how she'd look with bangs, and then couldn't get the brush unrolled. Miss Zona Clark had to cut her bangs so short, Jo Lynn cried and said she couldn't go anywhere until they grew out some. But Mama helped her make pincurls, two half circles of hair pointing at each other across her forehead like horns. I did not tease her.

Before Goose came to pick Jo Lynn up, Map and I left for the movies; I think Jo Lynn asked Map to get me out of the way. We saw *Oklahoma*, which was a love story with a little kissing and a lot of singing. The bad guy in it was a lot like Mr. B.Z., only bigger. But there were some pretty horses, and Map bought popcorn and cola and said again she was sorry she'd lost her temper and slapped me, so I had a halfway good time. We got home just before ten o'clock, which was the latest I'd ever been out in my life.

"I was sitting out here listening to the silence," Mama called from the dark screened porch. "I'm not by myself very often—it feels kind of good."

We went in and listened with her, nobody talking much.

After a while Mama said, "This is a peaceful house. Living here's not bad."

Stretched out on the chaise longue, I let myself

get drowsy counting the nut-crushing noises Mama's rocker made on its backswing.

"I sure thought I could do enough with the trucks to hang on. Your friend Mr. Mose tried to help, Prin. He sent us all that last business we had."

After another long while she said, "Brian and I had such big plans. We were going to build up front on the road, a fine house like yours, Map. This was to be the foreman's house. We planned to put a shop where the garden is so we could work on the trucks."

I scratched a chigger bite and tried to think what the big flat garden space would look like with a shop and a gravel yard for the trucks.

"But there won't be any new house. And the wise thing for right now is to sell the trucks. Maybe with our savings and what we get for them, we can pay off the bank." Mama sighed. "I guess we'll always be salaried people."

Her chair rocked back, and back, and back, crushing nuts as I lost count and dozed off.

The night was hot and still, and the plastic chaise cover kept sticking to my sweaty legs, so I only half slept, shifting my legs now and then with a sound like a peeled-off Band-Aid. I was about to move to a cooler chair when I realized that Mama and Map were still talking softly, this time about Daddy.

"Do you know what they're doing to Brian?" Mama was saying.

"What?"

"Shu-u-u. Prin?" Mama asked in a normal voice. "Are you awake?"

I did not answer.

After a minute, she went on. "They've collapsed his right lung to let it rest. He's got needle marks all over his stomach right under his breastbone, where they pump air into his diaphragm to support his lung. Every Wednesday I go with him to have that done. He never says a word."

"Can they tell you anything at all?" Map asked in a loud whisper.

"X-ray shows the spots on his lungs are contained, maybe just a fraction smaller. It'll be another month or so."

"What did you find out at the railroad yesterday?"

"Our benefits run out the first of October. They'll hold a job, but he'll lose seniority."

"Lord, Lord," Map whispered.

"There's just so much going on right now. I've been thinking and thinking about how to handle it all."

"One thing at a time."

It was all I could do not to sit right up and tell them how upset I was. If Mama had told me what she told Map and not made me eavesdrop, I could have asked her how Daddy really was, and where the air went when it was pumped in. Why didn't it leak back out? And what if it all didn't work? What if he stayed sick for years and years?

I wished I could see for myself how sick Daddy was. Even if I did let Mama know I'd eavesdropped and heard everything, she still might not tell me the whole truth about him. If she thought it would scare me, she'd keep it a secret.

I was stirred up and wide awake, and when we finally went to bed, I couldn't sleep. I read until Mama made me turn off the light, then I listened out my window, hoping the horses would run by. Pretty soon headlights flashed at the top of our driveway, and Goose Jamison's car started down the hill, slow and quiet. I remembered how the boy and girl in *Oklahoma* had kissed and decided if Jo Lynn and Goose did it, I wanted to watch.

I slipped off my top bunk and tiptoed around to Jo Lynn's room, climbed on the foot of her bed, and looked out the window as Goose's car rolled to a stop beside the carport.

The roof light flicked on, doors opened and shut,

then he and Jo Lynn were walking close together into the porch light, talking low. I was surprised to hear Mary Faith's name, then Jo Lynn say something about feeling sorry for her, and Goose laughing. They were right up at the front door where I couldn't see or hear, so I climbed in the window and pressed my face against the screen to get closer.

The next thing I knew I was falling and twisting through the air, bouncing between the screen and bushes and ground. Silver and yellow lights whirled around each other, and I was burning all over like a hundred wasps had stung me. Light spilled out the window where the screen was missing. Mama's head was there, then it wasn't; Jo Lynn was somewhere crying, and Map and Goose Jamison and then Mama were yelling and picking things off me.

"Are you all right?" they asked over and over, but I didn't have the breath to answer. I hurt bad. I was scratched and stuck with screen wires and splinters of broken shrubs. There was a lump on my head, my lip was swelling, and my front tooth was loose.

"What were you doing in the window?" Map yelled. I did not answer, but put my arms around Mama's big hard stomach and hid my face. Her

arm came around my shoulders, I heard her saying to lift my feet, step up to the porch, to the
house, and then she laid me down on the sofa and
felt my arms and legs all over. She asked a thousand times if I thought I'd hurt anything inside
myself, and put iodine on the cuts and told me to
go to bed, all without saying another thing but "Are
you all right?"

JO LYNN WAS furious, saying how I'd embarrassed
her so she'd never be able to look Goose Jamison
in the eye again.

"You're always sticking your nose in other people's business, poking around where you're not
wanted," she yelled. "Well, you just keep it up
and see where it gets you, Miss Priss. You're asking for trouble!" Map took her side like always.

I was cut and banged up enough to stay in bed
two whole days, with nothing to do but think. I
thought about how sore Daddy must be with so
many needle holes in his stomach, and I kept
hearing Mama's sad voice saying she and Daddy
were selling the trucks and would always be salaried people.

I wondered if Daddy was as upset about the
trucks as she was. Then I wondered if he even
knew. Mama might try to keep that a secret from

him like she tried to keep how sick he was from me, so I wouldn't worry. And even if Daddy knew about the trucks, had she told him that Mr. B.Z. was bothering us?

That led to thinking about Mary Faith. I hadn't seen her in a long time, and I wondered if she missed me, and if Mr. B.Z. was still treating her so mean.

On the third day I was glad to feel good enough to get up. Mama sent Map and Jo Lynn to the Crosstown Sears to pick up a catalogue order, and as soon as they left the house, I told Mama I was feeling better.

"Does everything work all right? Do you hurt especially bad anywhere inside?" Mama said, fixing me a peanut-butter-and-raisin sandwich and a glass of tea. I told her everything was fine except for the little finger of my left hand, which I'd landed on and jammed. "You take it easy for a few days," she said. "I don't want you tearing open any of those cuts and getting infected."

She went back to bed. I wanted to talk to somebody, so when I heard hammering over at Mr. Mose's, I walked over.

"You fall in a briar patch?" he said right off.

"Just about."

"Fall off your horse?"

"No, sir."

"Get caught in a buzz saw?"

"No, sir." I climbed over the fence and up on the truck fender with Joe Leonard.

Mr. Mose watched me, his long arm swinging a hammer like a clock pendulum. "Well, if you don't want to talk about it, that's all right with me. Most people think the most interesting thing in the world is other people's business, but I'm not that nosy." He went back to work, still watching me from the corner of his eye.

Then down near the road I saw a new wooden gate set in the fence between our place and his.

"It ain't as heavy as it looks," he said, pleased I'd noticed. "I put a rope loop on top you can just lean over and slip off. You won't even have to get off your pony to open it."

The cuts on my face hurt when they stretched, but I still smiled at him.

"B.Z. Hammond won't have any excuse to bother you now," he said right out. "I already told him to stay away from me and mine. I understand your mama's done the same."

"Yes, sir," I mumbled. Mr. B.Z. was too personal to talk about with Mr. Mose.

So I changed the subject to something else that was on my mind: "What's salaried people?"

"What's that?"

"What does salaried people mean? Mama said she and Daddy would always be salaried people."

Mr. Mose looked down at our house, at the dump trucks parked in the garden. "Means you work for somebody else," he said. "There's just so much you'll be paid every month or every week for doing something somebody else tells you to and making their business work."

"Is that bad?"

"Depends on what you want. It means you never own the way you live. And when you're old, you have to live off the grace of your children and a little bit of retirement."

"Is working for the railroad and teaching school salaried?"

"Yep."

"Is dump trucking?"

"Not if you own the trucks."

"But Mama's selling them. They're costing more than she can make, just herself."

Mr. Mose sighed. "I guess your mama ain't dreaming no more. She's lost something it's hard to live without."

I felt tired. My cuts were stinging, my little finger ached, and knowing Mama had given up a dream made me feel as bad inside as I did out.

Through the shade tree the heat beat on my shoulders and head, smothering me so I didn't even want to sit up.

"You better get on home," Mr. Mose said. "You look like the wrath of God warmed over. You want me to drive you?"

"No, sir."

He helped me over the fence. I could feel him watching me walk slowly across our pasture.

Twelve

I WAS GOING to the hospital to see Daddy. I had to talk to him. Even if he was sick, he needed to know that bad things had started the day he went into the hospital, and now they were all closing in.

So on Wednesday night I tried to eat supper like always, but Mama still asked did I feel all right. Finally she laid her knife and fork across the back of her plate. "Time for me to go," she said, and shoved back her chair.

I waited until she was in her bedroom getting her purse; then I said, "I have to go to the bathroom." Instead, I slipped out the back door and hid in the back of Mama's car as close under the front seat as I could squeeze.

If she had looked at all, Mama would have seen me, but she got in the car still talking to Map in the house. She took forever to get the car started.

Mama drove slow. There wasn't any noise except her tires whining down that long, straight stretch of Coleman Road. From the floorboard I could see the edges of trees like torn paper against the sky. Thunderclouds were rolling in, just beginning to rumble.

It was a long way, over the Wolfe River Bridge and down Jackson Avenue, where the streetlights were already on. I could see the tops of buildings, the thick wires for stoplights and telephone lines, and the crossbars of poles flashing by. The back of my neck was on the hump in the floorboard; I was comfortable enough to sleep. At the viaduct between the L&N switchyard and the Purina plant, the cottonseed smell woke me up a little. The hospital wouldn't be far.

When Mama finally stopped the car and got out, I sat up and looked around at a big parking lot with rows of lights shining bright against the storm.

Mama was a little dark shape walking toward the hospital.

The West Tennessee Tuberculosis Hospital was huge. Its main doors were lit up with yellow inside light, and out from that bright spot the brick building went off in every direction. Its hundreds of windows spit flares of light or were dark as shut eyes.

I followed Mama a ways back. She went in the door and nodded at somebody off to the side, then walked across the lobby to an elevator and disappeared. I ran through the doors and down the lobby, and got to the elevator just as its needle stopped at three. It started moving again, up, just as somebody started yelling and yanking my arm almost out of its socket.

"What're you doing?" I yelled, but she was a horsefaced woman who only *asked* questions. She dragged me along, not even looking at me until I stepped on her foot. Then she stopped, sucking her breath in and going bug-eyed.

"Excuse me," I said.

"Just what do you think *you're* doing?" Her arms cocked out like turkey wings. The white cap pinned on top of her head was about to shake off. "What do you think—*where* do you think you're going?"

"To see my daddy. He's Mr. Brian Campbell and I'd like to know what room he's in, please."

"You can't go up there," she said, her mouth all puckered up. "Only children twelve years old or older and accompanied by an adult can." She pointed at a sign on the wall that said all those things.

"I'm little for my age," I said.

"I doubt that. Where's your mother?"

"She just went up in the elevator. She told me to come on up soon's I's through in the bathroom."

"Sit down." She pointed at a chair. I sat on the edge of the seat while she marched off to a counter. Her eyes fixed on me so I couldn't move while she telephoned. I watched her talk, then watched the elevator doors, waiting for Mama.

I didn't care that I was in trouble, because I'd already decided I would pay what I had to to see Daddy. That's how bad I needed to talk to him about what was happening at home. I was still trying to figure out how to get to him when the elevator doors opened and Mama walked out.

The nurse shot across the lobby, her and Mama getting to me at the same time.

"You know she can't come in here," the nurse

said, loud. Everybody in the lobby stopped to watch.

"I know," Mama said, quiet. She stood straight, a lot shorter than the nurse, who was bending over her. "She just misses her daddy."

"It's the rules," the nurse said. "She can't come in here."

"She can't go *up there*," Mama said, a little louder. "This is a public lobby."

"Children have no place at a tuberculosis hospital. I'm surprised at you bringing her here."

"Don't be. There's sometimes things more important than rules, and she needed to see where her daddy is. All she's going to do is sit and wait."

"She tried to go up."

"You can't do that, Prin." Mama was talking to me, but looking straight at the nurse. The nurse was silent for a minute, not wanting to back down, but she did. I knew how fierce Mama's eyes were.

Just as soon as her back was turned, Mama dropped into the seat beside me. She stared at the wall with her face sad. "You could have scared me to death," she said. "I didn't know anybody was in the car."

I gave it one more try. "Why not?" I said. "Why can't I go up there?"

157

Mama sighed. "I've told you, tuberculosis is catching. It's especially bad on little people, so they can't go up and be exposed to it. If it wasn't catching, Daddy'd be at home right now. I'll tell him you came."

The nurse was watching us. Mama patted me on the arm so she could see, then walked over to the elevator and was gone.

She stayed with Daddy a long time. I sat awhile, spit on the chair arms and rubbed them clean, then wandered around the lobby, picking dust off the plastic plants and looking in all the ashtrays. Finally I leaned with the top of my head against the marble wall to see if I could be a straight slanted line without my feet sliding out from under me.

"Prin?"

My feet slipped. On my hands and knees I looked over at Mama standing just inside the elevator door with one finger on the button and another on her lips. Daddy was standing beside her.

I looked at the nurse, glad she was far enough away not to see my face or hear my breath coming in short little spurts. She watched me get up and dust off, and looked away when I walked slow, one hand on the wall, to just in front of the elevator.

Daddy had on house slippers and an old blue

robe and pajamas. His hair was gray at the sides, pressed tight and swirled like lying down does hair, with a cowlick sticking up in back. His skin was white and thin. He looked old and sick. He grinned at me, pointed at the lobby, and said, "Where's the nurse?" with no sound.

She was on the phone with her back to me.

"Okay," I said.

"Come quick." Daddy knelt down with his arms out, and I ran and hugged him, hiding my face in his shoulder. He smelled like a closed room where old people live, with a little sweet shaving smell on his cheek. He felt thin, bony in the shoulders; his hug was weak. He breathed hard. I remembered that the needle holes in his stomach would hurt with me mashing on them, and I pulled back. "No," he said, and rested with his chin on my shoulder.

"That's enough," Mama whispered.

"Scoot," he said.

"Wait, I need to talk to you," I said. But the doors were already shut.

In the ladies' room I locked the door so nobody could come in, and splashed my face with cold water until I was through crying. Then I went back to the lobby and sat down. When the nurse looked at me, I crossed my eyes at her.

In a little while Mama came down. She looked tired. "Let's go home," she said, putting an arm around my shoulder and cutting her eyes at the nurse.

In her other arm she carried her purse and some magazines; a pleated white paper cup on top was mashed against her chest. "What's that?" I said.

"Oh, my word." She looked at the crushed cup like it was going to bite her. "I meant to throw that away. Something your daddy sent you." The cup had two corn candies and a candy orange slice and a cookie with M&M's in the center. Before I could reach for it, Mama walked over to a trash can and dropped it in.

"What're you doing?" I yelled.

"No you don't." She caught my arm. "You can't have that—it's contaminated."

"Daddy sent it to me."

"You can't have it. It'll make you sick. Come on."

She held my arm tight, like the nurse had, and dragged me across the lobby and out the door. She kept hold down the steps and across the circle drive and the grass, out to a flagpole that had ropes flapping against it in the wind. "Now quit crying and look." She pulled me around and pointed up through the first drops of rain. "There's Daddy."

At one of the windows way up the little black shape of a person was there, a silhouette. It was thick black like the shadows of real things against a night sky, and it waved at us and Mama waved back. I waved, too, but it could have been anybody.

Thirteen

AT BREAKFAST THE next morning Map shot me a sor-
rowful look, and Jo Lynn said, "Well, now aren't
you sorry you went, Miss Smart Aleck?"

She was right. I did wish I hadn't seen Daddy
so sick; if Lady ran away with me now, he wouldn't
be able to stop her. He couldn't do anything about
what was going wrong at home, either.

I kept out of everybody's way as much as I could
that morning, and all afternoon I hid out in a lean-

to I'd made in the woods behind the barn. The horses came up to see what I was doing; Flash let me lie on her back, my legs and arms dangling, while she slept. After a long quiet while, Lady eased over and stood facing the opposite direction from Flash so she could switch flies around Flash's head. We three stayed close and quiet like that all afternoon, with Big Red sleeping a little ways off. By suppertime the sky was clear and I was feeling some better.

I did not try to wake up that night, but I did. A big gold moon blinked now and then at thin little clouds; I lay watching it and listening for the horses. After a while I unlatched the screen and slid out, thinking I'd feel all the way good if I did a little night riding.

The horses were grazing up front near the road. I cut through the mimosas and straight up the driveway, thinking how good the earth smelled and the air felt against my skin. Then Big Red's head came up; he swung around on his front legs, look-ing straight into the dark row of pine trees be-tween us and the Hammonds.

I stopped. But there was no sound coming from the Hammonds', no light winking through the pines, and after a while Red quit dancing and blew out his nose. When I moved again, he swung his head sharp toward me, alert for anything coming at him in the night.

I clicked my tongue, leaning on the fence talking to him. "Say, boy. Here, Big Red. It's me."

He watched me.

"Come on, boy." I kept talking till he lost interest, then slipped between the bottom two strands of wire and walked out into the pasture. I didn't have any trouble walking right up to Flash and getting on.

All of a sudden Red wheeled around on his back legs and snorted. His tail came up and he was off, galloping hard toward the lower pasture, his head darting out with each step. Lady was right behind him.

I wound my hands into Flash's mane, and she started off at a gallop, and in a minute the three of them were strung out across the field like beads on a string.

Flash's mane whipped up and stung my arms; my legs could feel her bones work back and forth under her skin. When she got into the trees I lay low, my arms around her neck while she raced downhill. Then we were in the back pasture, Big Red way ahead, sweeping up the hill toward the barn. He and Lady were lost for a minute, galloping through the valley under Mama's bedroom window and off to the left toward Mr. Mose Hardy's place.

That valley under Mama's window was the bad part. If she was watching, she couldn't miss seeing me, but there wasn't any way I could jump off in the dark. I hung on, still lying low, and Flash rounded the water trough and ran through the valley, blowing hard. When she saw that Red and Lady had stopped up in the front pasture, she slowed to a trot.

I didn't get off, just pushed back to Flash's broad, flat rump, waiting for my blood to slow down and watching Red and Lady. Flash grazed along, working her way up the hill, her rump tilting me from side to side every time she took a step. I felt good—washed clean by the horses and the warm night wind, and more at ease in my mind than I'd been in a long time.

Then from the trees on my left came a sound that snapped my head around. Mr. B.Z. Hammond stepped from the shadows and walked toward us, laughing and saying, "I seen you out here night riding. I knowed it was you. You think you can fool me with a lie?" He held an apple for Flash and walked slow and easy so as not to spook her.

A jolt shot through me, my breath stopped,

and my mind couldn't think. I just sat and stared while Flash reached for the apple and Mr. Hammond's hand clamped around a handful of her mane.

"It's time you and me got acquainted," he said. "I got some things for you you're gonna like."

When he reached for me I didn't think, but kicked Flash hard in the flanks. She jumped forward, shoving Mr. Hammond backward and rolling me off the end of her rump. I hit the ground rolling, too stunned to feel hurt, and came up on my feet in time to see Mr. Hammond lunge forward. He caught me by the arm and fell, pulling me down on top of him. I heard his breath whoosh out, felt his hold on my arm loosen, and I pushed backward, one foot then the other pounding against his rib cage until he let go. In a second I was up and running, heading up the pasture toward the horses because Mr. B.Z. was already on his feet between me and the house.

Way beyond the horses somebody else was running, too, coming toward us and screaming, "Stop it! Don't you touch her!" and in between, Lady and Flash were whirling in circles and Red was rearing up and screaming a strange, mean whinny.

Lady and Flash bolted down the hill to my right, but not Red. He did what he'd do to anybody who scared him in the night. He ran straight at me and Mr. Hammond.

I jumped sideways. Red thundered past and collided with Mr. Hammond, flipping him backward through the air like a bunch of rags. Red didn't stop or slow down, didn't rear up or kick or throw his front feet out. He just rolled Mr. Hammond over and over, screaming that strange whinny, then kept right on running, leaving Mr. Hammond a still heap in the moonlight.

Mr. Hammond had screamed, too, the awfulest sound I ever heard. It cut off quick, and for a split second there wasn't any noise but a soft wind rustling the grass and me crying. Then Mary Faith was running up between me and her daddy, looking from one to the other like she didn't know where to go first.

From inside Mr. Mose's camper Joe Leonard let out a high-pitched bay. He and Mr. Mose came slamming out the door, Mr. Mose's flashlight shooting darts of light in all directions. Down at our house Mama's light came on too.

Joe Leonard put his paws up on the chickenwire fence and pointed his nose right at Mary Faith and me. He howled, and Mr. Mose's flashlight turned in our direction. "Run!" Mary Faith pulled me up and shoved me toward the house.

I raced straight down the hill, my feet tangling in the high summer grass and tripping me over twice. Finally I reached the house and skinnied up the pin oak outside my window. Every light we had was on, and through the living-room window I saw Mama holding Daddy's big shotgun under her arm and Map coming in the front door.

The light made me miss a hold on a limb, and I slipped, skinning my knee and the knuckles of my left hand. But I managed to flip the screen out and climb inside and was rolling onto my bunk just as Mama came running down the hall. She flicked on my light and yelled for everybody to come to the living room.

"What's happened?" Jo Lynn was screaming from her room.

Mama didn't look at me, but ran as fast as she could down the hall to lock the back door. That gave me time to wipe my face on a corner of the sheet and then wrap up in it, I was shivering so bad. "Get in the living room, I said," Mama yelled, racing by my door again.

I made my legs walk to the big armchair and stood behind it with my hands clamped over its back to stop them shaking. Map was screaming into the telephone. I fixed my eyes on her to try to stop things from swimming around. I didn't feel any of the cuts or scrapes I knew were on me, didn't hear what Mama was saying until she shook me by the shoulder and snapped, "You girls get in Jo Lynn's closet."

"The sheriff's coming," Map screamed, hanging up the phone. "He's on his way."

"I said you girls get in the closet!" Mama yelled. We did, me huddling in a corner under Jo Lynn's skirts trying to stop shivering, and Jo Lynn hanging out the door watching.

"I hope this isn't a wild goose chase," Map squeaked.

"I heard a scream," Mama said. "Something spooked the horses."

"Look, there's somebody up in the pasture," Map yelled. "There's a light moving around up by Mose Hardy's."

"Don't you leave that closet," Mama called, and Jo Lynn drew back in a little.

"What do you suppose is going on? Who do you suppose that is?" Map said.

"Shu-u-u!" We all heard it, a car coming down the driveway. There were static voices from outside, and a faint red light pulsed around Jo Lynn's room. "Sheriff's office. Anybody home?" a man's voice called out.

"I hear you," Mama yelled back. "Up in the pasture there on your left."

"You stay right there," he said. "I'll send somebody down to check around the house soon's another car gets here."

The car backed up, its lights fading from Jo Lynn's walls. Mama called, "We're all right now. You girls come on in here."

I stood behind the chair again. Jo Lynn sat on the sofa by Map, her eyes so big the whites showed on all sides. "What is it?" she whispered. "What's going on?"

"Something's happened out in the pasture." Mama was looking at me; her nose wrinkled up, then flared out at the bottom. "How can you always manage to smell like horse?" she said. "Why are you all wrapped up in that sheet?"

She put a hand on the back of the sofa, staring at my bleeding knuckles. Her face went white. She leaned the shotgun against a chair; it slid down and banged to the floor, but she didn't pick it up. "Dear God in heaven," she whispered.

She walked quick to me, catching me by the shoulder and turning me around, marching me down the hall to my bedroom. She shut the door behind us.

"Now let go of that sheet." She caught one edge and pulled, and saw the dirt and grass stains on my pajamas, the blood already drying a fold of sheet to the skinned place on my leg. But her eyes fixed on my upper arm, where a purple bruise the size of Mr. Hammond's hand was already swelling. "What happened out there?" she whispered.

"I was night riding, and Mr. B.Z. came over—" My teeth chattered against each other; then I was shaking all over and Mama was on her knees holding me. Mama felt warm and strong and safe, and she held me till hiccups was all that was left of my crying. "It's all right, Princess," she said. "Nobody's going to hurt you now, I'm right here."

She held a corner of the sheet to my nose so I could blow, like she had when I was little. Then she said, "I need to know what happened, Prin—*everything* that happened."

"Mr. B.Z. was up in the pasture and Red hurt him," I managed to get out.

"Did B.Z. hurt you?"

I pointed at the bruise.

"Did he do anything else?"

"No, ma'am."

"Tell me the truth, now, Prin. Tell me everything."

"I am. He was chasing me and Red ran over him and Mary Faith told me to come home before Mr. Mose got there. I think he's hurt bad, Mama."

"Mary Faith was there, too?"

I nodded. "She tried to stop him."

"And he did stop? That's *all* he did to you, that bruise?"

I nodded again.

Mama's eyes squeezed shut. She gripped my hands so hard I thought they'd break.

"Get on some clean pajamas," she said, bracing herself on the bottom bunk and getting to her feet. Her face was still white. "Stuff those dirty pajamas under your pillow—we'll get rid of them later. Hurry," she said, yanking open a dresser drawer and digging through my things until she came up with a long-sleeved nightgown. I edged over and pulled it easy out of her fingers.

"Ada Ruth, there's a car coming," Map was calling from the living room.

"Don't you say a word out there," Mama said, her eyes going from my top bunk to the window. "Don't you say one word until this is over. Do you hear me?"

"Yes, ma'am."

"Not a word."

We went back into the living room and waited with Map and Jo Lynn while cars crunched down our driveway and red and white and yellow lights spattered outside our windows. "You all right in there, ma'am?" a man called. Mama yelled we were, and we listened while two or three men walked all around the house talking to each other.

Mama pulled me against her side, and I rested there, my eyes closed. "Prin's scared," she explained to Map and Jo Lynn. "I guess we're all scared." She kissed the top of my head and whispered, "Did you get the screen closed?" and I nodded against her.

Then somebody was banging on the front door and calling out. Mama went to answer, leaving a cool place on my cheek where it had rested against her. She opened the door and stood in it so I could just see the top of a man's hat, flat brimmed and muddy colored in the yellow porch light.

"Ma'am, there's a man been hurt up in your pasture, run down by something." He stopped talking a minute, but Mama didn't say anything. "I can't figure what he was doing up there, now, can you?"

"No." Mama's voice was dead calm.

"It don't make sense, the dead of night, for him to have any business up there, unless he was molesting your animals some way. You got animals?"

"Horses."

He nodded. "There's tracks."

He waited again, but Mama didn't say anything.

"He's hurt real bad."

She didn't say anything.

"Ever'body here all right?"

"Yes."

"Ever'body been here all night?"

"Yes."

"Who-all's here?"

"Me. My sister-in-law. My two girls."

"You hear anything?"

"I heard a scream."

"What about you, ma'am?" He was calling around Mama to Map.

"I didn't hear anything. I didn't hear a thing," Map whispered.

"What kind of scream was it?"

"Just a scream," Mama said. "The horses had been restless."

"You think something was disturbing them?"

"They run sometimes at night." Mama leaned against the doorframe.

"How come you suppose that is?" the man said.

"I don't know. I don't have any idea."

"My men walked around the pasture. Course the horses is so skittish they won't let anybody near right now. It's a mighty big horse that'd run down a grown man. You got a big one?"

"Yes, Big Red."

"He pretty mean?"

"No, I—he's just a horse."

"You girls see anything?" He was peering around Mama's shoulder.

"No. The girls were asleep. I had to wake them up," Mama said.

"That right, girls?" he called.

Jo Lynn nodded. So did I.

He stepped back. "Well, ma'am, I reckon I'll leave a man here tonight, if you don't mind. Just a precaution. In the morning I'll need to come look at the horses. I can't think why that man'd be out in the pasture in the middle of the night. It don't make sense."

"No." Mama was just whispering. "Who is it?"

He was quiet for a long time, till I thought he wasn't going to answer. "Looks like it was your neighbor B.Z. Hammond," he said.

Mama's hand went to her mouth.

"Did he ever ride those horses?" the sheriff said.

"Ever show any interest in them, one way or other?"

"No, he never did."

"Mighty strange." He stepped back, putting a finger to the brim of his hat and backing off the porch.

They all left but one car. We sat in the living room without talking or moving until they had gone. The bruise on my arm was beginning to throb, and I was stinging all over from horse sweat and grass, and all the cuts and scratches I'd gotten falling down.

I was so tired I had to fight to stay awake, and my chin had almost dropped to my chest when Mama said, "Go back to bed now, everybody. It'll be daylight soon enough, and us with no sleep. Map, you stay with Jo Lynn. Prin'll sleep with me."

I dragged myself to Mama's room and lay down, glad for the feel of pillows and sheets to wrap up in. Mama moved around awhile in my room, then walked past the door with my sheet and pajamas in her hand. She turned on the washing machine, left the hall light on, and came to bed, lying straight back. She put her arm out and said, "Come over here."

I moved close, put my arm over her belly, and felt the baby moving. Mama's shoulder was warm and soft; her fingers rubbed up and down my good arm. "I wasn't paying attention," she said, sounding far away. "I could have saved you a lot of grief if I'd quit feeling so sorry for myself and just paid attention."

"I just wanted to be Mary Faith's friend," I mumbled, fighting to keep my eyelids open.

"I suspect she's needed one. Go to sleep now," Mama whispered, her soft hand rubbing my arm. "We'll talk tomorrow."

Fourteen

THE NEXT MORNING I was clean, my leg was bandaged, and the horse sweat and dirt and grass stains had been washed off me. I put on the blue jeans and long-sleeved shirt Mama had laid out and watched through the window with Map and Jo Lynn while the sheriff and his deputies looked Big Red over. They had a strap around his neck, and he stood quiet while they picked up his hooves one at a time. They looked at Lady's feet, too, but just petted Flash. The sheriff talked with Mama a long time out in the yard.

"What'd they say?" Map said when Mama came in. "What'd they find out?"

"They think it was Red."

"I could have told them that," Map said.

"Let's all sit at the table," Mama said. She sat pushed back, leaving room for her belly, and put her hands flat on the table, fingers spread.

"A terrible thing has happened," she said, looking at each of us. "A man's been killed on our place by one of our horses. It was an accident." She looked at me. "I don't know what he was doing in our pasture. Maybe he was drunk, or maybe he'd got lost, something had happened to his mind, and he was where he didn't have any business being. Maybe he was just out walking. I don't know."

I stared at my hands and listened to Mama change what had happened, telling it so nobody would ask me anything about Mr. B.Z. or know I had been night riding.

"All I know is he got hurt being where he ought not have been, and he's died from it." She looked at each one of us again. "It's a terrible thing."

She said real low, "Poor Mary Faith."

Map straightened her back. Before she could say

anything, Mama said, "I want you to make a meat loaf, Map, some butter beans, and cornbread. We'll take it up to those children."

Map's mouth opened.

"And you call the church, see if the Rebekkah Class wants to do something. Those children have to get through this thing too."

"What about Red?" I said.

"That horse'll have to be put away," Map said. "He's a killer."

"He was where he ought to be. B.Z. Hammond wasn't."

"Mama, Red was trying to—"

"Be quiet, Prin."

"You can't keep a horse that's a killer. Not with children."

"That's for the sheriff to decide. Not you, not me." Mama's eyes snapped at Map.

"We don't have any cornmeal," she said, sniffing. "I'll have to go to the store before I can even make cornbread. I'll get my purse." She got up slow.

"Go with her," Mama told Jo Lynn.

Jo Lynn went.

"Let's go sit on the swing," Mama said to me.

Outside, Mama looked at the horses in the valley, her eyes roving up the hill where it had all happened, then over to the tree outside my window.

"Prin, some things need to be said. I don't know if you can understand all of this right now, but you need to know the truth.

"I went over up to see Mary Faith this morning early, to thank her for trying to help you last night. She told me what I'd already guessed, that B.Z. was the father of her baby. Do you understand what I'm saying?"

"Yes, ma'am," I mumbled, wishing I didn't.

"I'm talking about incest, Prin; about a man having sex with his daughter. It's not love, but a kind of violence, a way for a weak man like B.Z. to show that he's stronger than his child, and force her to do whatever he wants."

"Did he hurt her bad?" I whispered.

"I'm sure he did, in her mind as well as her body. It'll be hard for Mary Faith to feel good about herself when her own father, who's supposed to love her, mistreated her so. She'll be ashamed about what's happened to her even though she's not to blame for any of it."

I rested my face against Mama's shoulder, not wanting to know any more.

Mama went on, her arm around me. "Last night B.Z. would have done to you what he did to Mary

Faith, if Red hadn't hurt him." She shook her head, her face grim. "I'm not real concerned about what happened to B.Z. Hammond; he's probably the worst person any of us'll ever know. Now he's paid for it. I just wish Mary Faith and you weren't going to have to pay for it, too."

I knew right away how Mary Faith was paying, and when I thought about it, I knew how I was. B.Z. Hammond had brought something bad to the house next door, then to our front gate, and finally onto our place itself. I didn't think I could ever feel safe again.

I had already heard too much bad news. But there was still one thing Mama hadn't said. "What'll happen to Red?" I asked.

"That's for the sheriff to decide."

"He's Daddy's horse."

Mama tucked a strand of hair into my braid. "There's nothing your daddy can do about this, Prin, not even if he were here. This is up to the sheriff."

"But if we tell him why Red—"

"We're not going to tell him anything. Red is just a horse; you and Mary Faith are children.

"You and I won't pretend to each other that nothing happened—that would be a lie. It would be harder, sometime when you're all grown up, if we don't talk about it now. Do you understand that?''

''Yes, ma'am.''

Mama smiled a little. ''Here's the catch,'' she said. ''Only you and I and Mary Faith will ever know about it, because we're not going to tell anybody else. Can you do that?''

''Yes, ma'am.''

''Telling would hurt people more, would be real ugly. And I expect Mary Faith and her brother have enough to live with. We do too.''

The morning was hot. There wasn't any air stirring, and the sun glared down too bright, too clear and yellow.

''It'll go on for a while,'' Mama said. ''People will say things to us—to you—about Red. Don't answer.''

Mama grunted. ''That rascal kicked me,'' she said, patting her stomach. Her arm tightened on my shoulder. ''The baby's big enough to be born now and be all right, so Map'll be leaving soon. Then, before you know it, the summer will be over and Daddy'll be coming home and we'll be a family again. That's how things go on.'' She slid to the front of the swing and braced herself to stand up.

''What about my special thing?'' I asked, needing to have something good come from all that had happened. "You promised Jo Lynn and me one good and special thing this summer. I haven't had mine."

"What do you want?"

"I want Mary Faith to come live with us."

Mama sank back into the swing. After a few deep breaths she said, "I don't want Mary Faith to live here. I don't want any more of her hurt to rub off on you. Mary Faith knows things I hope you never know, and I'm going to protect you from them as long as I can."

"But Mama—"

"The answer is no, Princess." Slow tears slid down Mama's face. "That's a hard thing for me to say about somebody who's been good to you, but it's the truth. You'll understand better someday when you have girls of your own to take care of. You choose something else for your good and special thing."

Fifteen

LATE THAT MORNING we carried the cornbread and butter beans and meat loaf up our long driveway to the Hammonds'. Jo Lynn and Map said they were sorry and was there anything we could do, but seeing Mary Faith upset me so bad I couldn't say anything at all. I wanted to get her alone and talk about it, but in front of Map and Jo Lynn I didn't open my mouth. Mary Faith must have felt the same way, because both of us stared at the wall or the floor and never once looked each other in the eye.

We were the first ones there except for Mr. Mose and our preacher, Dr. Patterson. They were outside talking to Larry about funeral arrangements and saying the church would take up a donation. Next came a lady I didn't know who was the county social worker asking if Mary Faith and Larry had any relatives they could go live with. She said some grownup from the welfare department would come over to stay the night, and then she left.

Map and Jo Lynn began to clean up the kitchen and fix something to eat for Mary Faith and Larry, while Mama took Mary Faith off to the living room for a talk. I hung around the corner watching, but they never did ask me to come in. Mary Faith looked at her hands and nodded at what Mama was saying. When Mama grunted and patted her belly, Mary Faith asked her something, and Mama took Mary Faith's hand and put it on the baby. Mary Faith's whole body went quiet, her head dropped like she was listening to a whisper, and she kept her hand there for a long time. I remembered her saying how much she wanted her baby so she would have somebody to take care of and be hers, and my heart nearly broke.

When the ladies started coming, Mama gathered us in the dining room and put her arms

around my and Jo Lynn's shoulders. We stood together against a wall, Map tucking herself in behind Mama. There were lots of people bringing
things—the four of us, Mrs. Otwell, the principal
and two schoolteachers from Bartlett High that Jo
Lynn had called, Mama's Sunday school class, and
some Methodist ladies. They looked at us from the
corners of their eyes, touched Mama's arm, and
spoke as softly as if somebody in our family was
dead too.

Mary Faith sat at the kitchen table wearing short
shorts and an old shirt, looking surprised that her
house was filling up with people. Her face was
scrubbed; her hair was clean and straight and had
a lot of dark roots showing. She didn't have on
any makeup. She stared at the plate of food she
was nibbling on and didn't say a word to anybody, looking real uncomfortable. Every once in a
while she would sneak a look at me like she was
asking a question.

I tried to help out. I said, "Mary Faith paints
pictures—she's real good. She painted a picture of
Big Red that Daddy would like."

Everybody shifted feet, but nobody asked to see
it.

"I bet she could sell her paintings," I said.

But nobody picked up on it. The Methodist la-

d around the kitchen, trying to find a
the refrigerator for what people had
Mary Faith didn't know the social graces
〝 thank you or telling anybody where to
put things.

"I got a new picture to show you," she said to
me all of a sudden. She took my hand and led me
down the hall to her room, shut the door, and stood
with her back to it.

I faced her, feeling strange remembering how
the last time I'd been in this room Mr. B.Z. had
barged in unzipping his pants. Mary Faith had
jumped between us, and she'd worked to get me
away from him. She'd come to help me again last
night, too.

"Thank you for trying to save me from your
daddy," I blurted. "I know what he did to you.
He'd have done it to me, too, if he could've." My
throat closed tight.

Mary Faith hung her head and looked ashamed,
lifting things and putting them down where they
had been.

"What he did was his fault, not yours," I tried
again, needing to help her feel better. "You don't
have to feel ashamed."

"I cain't talk about none of that right now," she
whispered, crumpling a painting in her fist.

"There's all these ladies out there wanting to know what's been going on, and I cain't let it show. I cain't talk now!"

"All right, we don't have to talk about it. Show me your new picture," I said, putting an arm around her to calm her down.

"I don't have one," she whispered, resting her head against mine. "I just wanted to get out of there."

After a while she quit trembling and straightened up. "I ought to give you that picture of Red. I don't guess I can keep it now—that wouldn't seem right." She looked at it a long time, touched Red's nose with her finger. "It's the best thing I ever done."

She gave it to me.

"What are you going to do?" I said. "Where will you live?"

"A foster home, I guess." She shrugged. "I been in one before. But it won't be for long—I can move out when I'm eighteen. Larry's joining the army. He'd been meaning to anyway."

She sat on the edge of her bed, pulling at her shorts. "Tell me what to wear. What should I put on?" she said.

"A skirt, I guess. Maybe something you wear to school."

She pulled two or three skirts out of the closet, put on a dark one and a white blouse.

"You look real good," I said. "You're real pretty."

She almost smiled. "What do I say to those ladies? How do I talk to them? I hadn't never talked to grown-up women before."

"Well, you say yes ma'am and thank you, things like that."

"For what?"

"It doesn't matter. They expect it."

"Oh." She smoothed her skirt, pulled her socks up straight, and licked her lips. "I guess I better get back."

The ladies complimented her on her skirt and her hairdo, said not to worry, they'd take care of everything, and would she like a piece of cake. "Yes, ma'am, thank you," she said.

Mama tugged at my hand, and we slipped out the kitchen door and past the men standing around smoking. Mr. Mose walked a few steps with us. "I'm sure sorry about all this, Miss Ada," he said to Mama. "Seems like trouble comes in threes, don't it?" I guess he was thinking about Daddy and the trucks.

"Seems like," Mama said.

"There's anything I can do for you, you just let me know."

"I will."

"Miss Prin?"

I stopped and looked up at him.

Mr. Mose stooped down level with my eyes and held out his hand. "Are you all right?" He looked at me like he was searching for something, his warm hard hand holding mine in a grown-up handshake.

"Yes, sir, I'm fine."

"I'm sorry about Red."

"Yes, sir."

Mr. Mose stepped back and nodded at Mama, his eyes telling her something that made her nod back. He turned back toward the house, and we four walked up to the road and around to our own driveway.

At home I showed Mary Faith's picture to Mama. "Why, she is good," she said, and studied it a minute. "She's got a real talent. We'll get a frame at Woolworth's. You can hang that on your wall."

"It's for Daddy."

"Then we'll put it in his room when he gets home."

I WAITED FOR Mary Faith in the pine cave for days after the funeral, but she didn't come. Her old house looked like it was already empty, and I was afraid I would never see her again.

Then one morning after breakfast when I stepped out the kitchen door, she stepped out of the pines and waved, then turned back and disappeared. I didn't try to hide from anybody that I was going to see her, but ran up the middle of the driveway and crawled into the pines. "I've been waiting here every day for you," I said. "I was afraid you were gone for good."

She shot me a grateful look, then studied the ground again.

Finally she said in a rush, "I ain't sorry he's dead." Her face colored, her eyes teared up. "The social worker says I should be ashamed. She thinks I'm awful."

"You're not," I said. "She didn't know your daddy, she doesn't know how he gave you a baby, or pushed you down the stairs and things like that."

"How'd you know he pushed me?" she said, wiping at her face.

"I saw him. I was night riding, and heard some noise and came over to see what was going on. Before we were friends, I used to spy on you a lot."

She dropped her head to her knees, a big sob

shaking her shoulders. "He hit me all the time, but I never told nobody. I couldn't tell them that without telling them all the rest, and I was too ashamed. I didn't think anybody'd believe me anyway."

"It's hard to tell," I said. "But telling's important, because nobody can help you if they don't know anything's wrong." My eyes were tearing up, too, and I was sorry I didn't know how to say things as good as Mama did.

But gradually Mary Faith grew quieter, her sobs giving way to deep gulps and then to regular breathing.

"That night I woke up when I heard him leave the house," she finally said. "I followed him to the gate and seen him standing in the trees watching the horses, but I couldn't think what in the world he was up to. If I'd knowed he was waiting for you, I might could have warned you."

"You did what you could. You did just fine," I said. "He didn't hurt me bad, just bruised my arm a little."

She blew her nose on the corner of her shirt and straightened up to watch the social worker lady come out the front door with a suitcase. "You got a nice mama," she said, watching the lady plunk the suitcase down by the car, reach in the window, and honk the horn. "I hope your daddy is all right and gets to come home soon, too. I gotta go." She scooted toward the tunnel.

"Where do you think you'll be living?"

"I don't know. It's hard to find a place for girls as old as me. There might be a home in Millington that will take me. Nobody'll know about me there."

"Can I write to you?"

She turned and looked at me, eyebrows up. "Why?"

"I don't know," I said. "I just thought that'd be nice."

"I'm too old for you." She smiled, ducked her head, and started out under the pine branches.

"Wait a minute," I called. "How come the sheriff didn't know you were up in the pasture?"

She turned back a little. "Mr. Mose told me to go home," she said. "He said if I stayed, the sheriff would want to know what I was doing there, and then they'd find out about you. So I did, and when they come to tell me what had happened, I pretended I'd been asleep and didn't know a thing about it. I ain't ever going to tell anybody different."

"Me neither," I said.

Mary Faith backed out of the cave and squeezed through the barbed wire fence. Just one time her hand flipped a backward wave at me, and then she was gone.

THAT WAS A week ago. Last Sunday at church Sarah Chaney said I'd had the best summer of anybody, because something exciting had happened, and everybody would want to hear about it the first day of school. But I can't tell them what really happened. I don't even want to.

Mama once said that not telling the truth can sometimes be a social grace, that if we knew everything about each other, it would be hard to live together. She's right. Some things are too painful to know about each other, and there are times when telling the truth only hurts people more without changing a thing. What's happened will be my secret and Mama's, and Mary Faith's.

I talk about Mary Faith a lot with Mama, who says she has a good heart and a chance for a good life without her daddy. I think about how different my daddy is from B.Z. Hammond, and how that makes my own chances good and special.

School starts Monday. These last few days have come and gone and come and gone like the sound of the well pump kicking on and off, with a nice low hum. Our house feels like something good is about to happen. Daddy's coming home the first of September, but he'll have to stay in bed another six months to let his lungs heal. Map has moved out, leaving her bed and dresser so Daddy will have a quiet place to rest when the baby cries, and so she can come back and help.

The trucks are gone. Red is gone, too. The sheriff came for him the day after the funeral. I didn't ask and he didn't say what was going to happen.

I still ride Flash over every afternoon and talk to Mr. Mose and Joe Leonard. He has never said a word about that night. Sometimes I think Mary Faith was wrong, that he didn't know I was there, but then I remember the look he gave Mama, and the way he shook my hand like a grownup, and I know he does.

The old Thompson house is deserted again, with weeds peeking through the hard-packed ground that was the basketball court. That bare patch is the only sign that the Hammonds ever lived next door, that and the uneasy feeling I get every now and then. I feel like B.Z. Hammond has set something with night feet loose in our pasture. It's one of those thick darknesses that's gone when you look right at it, but moves in the corner of your eye when you look somewhere else. Mama has helped me nail shut the screen on my window so it can't get inside.

She's asked me if I'd like to get Daddy a new horse for my good and special thing. She may be right; a new horse could be just the thing, and it might help Daddy get well faster so we can go riding. I want a gelding as spirited as Big Red, who can make Lady and Flash want to run again.

And the next time I go night riding, I'll leave through the front door. I'll tell Mama I'm going, too, so she can watch from her window when we come racing through the valley and up the high front pasture, all silver and black shadows flying through the night.

Katherine Martin

was born in Memphis, Tennessee, and graduated from Mississippi College in Clinton, Mississippi. She lives on a quiet 20-acre ranch just outside the city with her husband, Robert. *Night Riding* is her first novel.

The character of Prin's mother, Ada Ruth, was inspired by Ms. Martin's own mother, to whom this book is a tribute.